# HE AIN'T DEAD

# HE AIN'T DEAD

### A Reed Haddok Western

## Tom Whatley

SUNSTONE
PRESS

SANTA FE

Sunstone books may be purchased for educational, business, or sales promotional use. For information please write: Special Markets Department, Sunstone Press, P.O. Box 2321, Santa Fe, New Mexico 87504-2321.

---

Library of Congress Cataloging-in-Publication Data:
Whatley, Tom., 1940–
    He ain't dead: a Reed Haddok western / Tom Whatley.
        p. cm.
    ISBN: 0-86534-344-6
    1. Arizona—Fiction. I. Title.

PS3573. H33 H4 2002
813′ .54—dc21                                    2002017682

---

SUNSTONE PRESS
Post Office Box 2321
Santa Fe, NM 87504-2321 / USA
(505) 988-4418 / *orders only* (800) 243-5644
FAX (505) 988-1025
**www.sunstonepress.com**

For Roslyn,
Steven, Stacy, and Jennifer

Somewhere in the distance a door slammed over and over in the howling wind. Rain crashed against the wall like muzzle blasts from a thousand scatter guns. Sleep would not come. However, the storm brought a certain assurance. Surely nobody would be out on a night like this, he thought.

But in the next moment there was the sound of footsteps in the hall outside. The handle turned and the door swung open. A flash of lightning briefly illuminated the room.

Falling out of the bed, Loyd Beecham crawled to the far corner of the room. He stared wild-eyed at the man standing in the doorway. He begged him to leave, then made incoherent promises that ended in a ear splitting scream.

It woke him up. Another dream. It was not raining and the night was still and quiet. The big man, wet from sweat and with a racing heart, rolled out of bed and poured himself a drink. With a shaky hand he raised it to his lips and gulped it down. Haddok has to die quick, he thought. This has got to stop.

## 1850s, somewhere in northern Arizona

The wind felt gentle against Reed Haddok's face. He sat his horse along the crest of a long ridge that ran across his range on the Rocking H ranch, watching his cowhands as they pushed the cattle out of the draws and thickets that ran back toward the mountains. He had spent long hours getting the ranch into working shape and preparing for the coming winter. Loyd Beecham had let the ranch go down while he owned it and Haddok was determined to make it a profit making business. The easiest part was running Beecham off. The hard part would be making the ranch work.

He had one bunch of cowhands gathering cattle and another building holding areas and laying in hay. The gather was going good and the cattle seemed in fair shape. He needed to put them on the best grass and get weight on them before winter. There was a lot of young stuff he was branding and weaning.

Haddok thought back over the days that had passed since he had taken over. Most of the ranchers who were forced off their land by Beecham had returned and they were working hard to get their ranches back in shape as well. They all held Haddok in high regard because he had been the reason they had their ranches back. He was their hero. They held meetings on a weekly basis to assist each other. Calm had returned to Prescott.

The one thing that had been a joy was Samantha. Their romance had gown stronger. He had visited the Diamond on four occasions and she had been to the Rocking H three times. They were comfortable with each other. Sam understood that Reed's attention had to be centered on the ranch for

9

the time being. Marriage was certain for them. It was just a question of time. Reed  wanted to have the ranch ready for her as much as he wanted it working and productive. The happiness that flooded his life was unlike anything he had ever known. He often thought to himself that he was the luckiest man alive.

Josh Spencer had fully recovered from his injury and was now working long and hard days alongside Reed as they whipped the ranch into shape. They would talk and plan at night and then oversee different jobs during the day. They were a team and it was obvious to all who knew them that their loyalty to each other was strong.

As Reed sat there watching the cowhands work, his emotions were a mixture of peace, fulfilment, and love. Sam was always on his mind. Owning a ranch like the Rocking H was a dream he had figured would never come true. Being free from having to look over his shoulder all the time, expecting someone to try and kill him, had become relaxing. Life couldn't be any better.

His attention drifted to a single puffy white cloud hanging over the mountain to his right. It resembled a horse running free as it bounced around in the updraft. He enjoyed the moment, not knowing that another cloud was rising.

Someone in New Mexico with a burning hatred was determined to see him dead. His days of peace would be brief. The love of his life would be severely tested. The Rocking H ranch would have to be defended.

But at the very moment he sat enjoying a simple cloud, plans were being placed in motion to take his life. Another unknown fact existed for those who would take money to murder a man. Reed Haddok would require a lot more killing than most folks.

## Santa Fe

He was curled up like a baby, his entire body shaking. Both he and his bed were wet from the sweat running off his body. The room was dark. Nobody could hear the infant whimper that came from his mouth. The night had been like all the rest and its terror had brought him from sleep to the reality of the helpless frightened man he had become. In this dream Haddok had been standing over him with his knife against his neck. He had been shamefully begging for his life when he woke up. This nightly trip through hell would never end until Haddok was dead.

Apart from his nightmarish nights, Beecham was gradually getting himself back into the mainstream of Santa Fe. He had been careful in constructing the alias. Nobody knew Loyd Beecham. Everyone knew Frank Lain to be a wealthy and influential business man.

His injuries had healed with no lasting scars. But his rage had not healed. He recalled the surge of joy and relief he felt the day he sent Ike Craven to kill Haddok. No man in the territory was a match for Craven. Haddok was as good as dead.

He had estimated it would be at least three weeks before he would hear from Craven and know for sure.

His immediate plan upon hearing of Haddok's death had been to gather a group of gunslingers and go back to Prescott to claim his property. Then three weeks had passed and he had heard nothing. He could not imagine what had gone wrong. Ike Craven was the best. He would just have to be patient and wait.

11

Thinking back, he rolled over and tried to sleep to crush those memories. It was useless. He crawled out of bed and walked over to his chair by the window. He wrapped a blanket around himself to shield him from the chill and allowed his hatred for Reed Haddok to burn in his heart.

His waiting had now lasted almost two months. There was a knock at his door..

"Come in," Beecham said loudly.

The door opened and Rosetta, his maid, walked in with an envelope. She extended it to him as she spoke. "This was delivered for you a moment ago." Beecham took the envelope as she turned to leave the room, closing the door behind her.

Beecham tore the envelope open and read its contents with shock and anger.

> F. Lain,
>
> Craven did not make it to Prescott. He was killed in a small town in New Mexico by and unknown gunman. I just heard it today. It is true. Haddok ain't dead.
>
> Will Malone

Beecham's hands trembled as he read and re-read the note. This just couldn't be. The best gunman he could find to kill Haddok didn't even make it to Prescott. It was unbelievable that so many things could go wrong.

He placed the note in his desk and sat down to think this thing through. He had to get rid of Haddok. There had to be a way. He began to write down the names of people he had used in the past, those who might be capable of killing Haddok. Most of the people he thought of he discarded because they could not have held a light to Ike Craven.

He spent most of the afternoon brooding. It was getting late when a plan began to emerge. He thought, if one man can't do it, I'll go with

12

numbers. I'll hire as many people as I can who will kill for money and send them all. Money was not a problem.

He walked to the door and called Rosetta. He told her to send Pablo to the Empire saloon to tell Will Malone he wanted to see him as soon as possible. After she departed, he sat down and began to write. He was excited just thinking about Reed Haddok being the target of a large number of hired killers. Haddok's luck was about to run out.

It was getting dark when Will Malone arrived. Malone was the only man in Santa Fe that knew Beecham's real identity. He had come to Santa Fe with Beecham when he left New Orleans. He served as Beecham's right hand man in all of his illegal dealings. As a gambler he was in the perfect place to keep up with all the news and to know all the unsavory people Beecham might need to call on.

"Pablo said you needed to see me," Malone said. "What you got going on?"

"I'm trying to put together a plan that will put an end to Reed Haddok," Beecham replied. "Take a look at this." Beecham handed Malone the sheet of paper he held in his hand. Malone read it.

> Twenty thousand dollars to whoever kills Reed Haddok
> of Prescott in the Arizona territory. Payment will be made
> upon proof of his death. Contact Loyd Beecham through
> Will Malone, Empire saloon, Santa Fe, New Mexico.

"That's a lot of money, Beecham," Malone said. "I might take this job myself."

"Believe me, you don't want this job. I want you to put this message out on the outlaw telegraph line. I know how they talk. It won't take long

13

before the word is out. I hope twenty thousand dollars will cause a hundred different killers to head for Prescott."

"It'll cause a stir all right. I'm not sure I've ever heard of that much money being placed on one man's head. This Haddok must have caused you a great deal of grief."

"He has. You will have to be careful and not let anybody tail you to me. From now until Haddok is dead we'll communicate through messages delivered by mouth. Nothing written. I'll send Pablo to the general store next to the saloon at noon each day. You can go there to buy your cigars at the same time. You can exchange any messages. If you have a need to get a word to me at another time, then send a runner to alert me and I'll send Pablo to the general store immediately."

"I can handle that. But why all the caution? Nobody in Santa Fe knows who you are and I'm not about to tell."

"We are dealing with a man that has an unusual ability to stay alive. He promised that if he ever heard of my whereabouts he would track me down and kill me. I don't want to look up some day and see him standing there."

"This sure is odd, Beecham. I've never known you to be afraid of any man."

"If you knew him like I know him, you would be afraid of him too. He's not like any man I've ever known. I'm not going to rest easy until I know he's dead."

"Well, this ought to do it. I'll get the word out and we'll just wait and see what happens. I'll be in touch and let you know if we get any takers."

Malone left the house and returned to the saloon and Beecham finally relaxed a bit and enjoyed the thought of Haddok being dead. However, he had an uneasy feeling. It seemed that every time he enjoyed thinking about Haddok being dead he kept hearing that he was alive.

Malone put the word out and the news spread quickly. The outlaws who heard it were shocked that anyone would pay that much to have a man killed. The price was tempting to them all. However, there was some more talk making the rounds in the saloons and hideouts. It was about Reed Haddok and how he had cleaned up Prescott single handed. The talk of fingers being cut off and a blazing draw that had left good gunmen dead tempered their desire to earn twenty thousand dollars.

Most of these men liked to pick their prey and they didn't like going up against a stacked deck. If Beecham was willing to pay that much, then there must be something about Haddok that warranted that price. Twenty thousand dollars was of no use to a dead man. So they mostly talked about the offer and decided to wait and see who would claim it.

*West Texas*

It was mid morning in the little town of Gurley. The man in the black coat was sitting in a straight backed chair in the corner of the blacksmith shop. He was thin as a whisper of smoke and his shoulders drooped. His eyes had a vacant look as they stared out over a hawk-like nose. He wore no pistol. He looked like a weasel.

While the blacksmith worked on replacing a shoe for his horse, the man took tobacco out of his coat pocket, deftly held the paper with his left hand and shook out an exact amount. He spread the tobacco carefully with his finger tips and rolled the paper in one easy motion. The cigarette was then lifted to his mouth where he licked the paper and smoothed it down. After twisting one end, he placed it in his mouth and lit it.

He breathed the smoke deep into his lungs and relaxed. This was a process he had repeated so many times in his life he could do it on the back of a running horse. Smoking was one of the few pleasures Reuben Partlow knew. He usually started the whole process all over again almost immediately.

The blacksmith broke the silence, continuing his work on the horse. "I guess you've heard all the talk going around about one of our Texas boys having a big price on his head out in Arizona?"

Partlow looked up. "Nope! What about it?"

"Well, a feller by the name of Haddok left out of east Texas a couple of years back." The blacksmith raised up from his work and wiped the sweat off his face as he talked. "He headed out west. He was just a kid it

16

seems, but he left here with a name for being hell on wheels when it came to trouble. They tell it that he landed in Arizona at a place called Prescott. It's being talked that he cleaned up a nest of gunslingers and run off a big time rancher and trouble maker by the name of Beecham. Beecham has landed in Santa Fe and is now offering to pay twenty thousand dollars to any man who kills Haddok."

"Twenty thousand dollars," said Partlow. "Why, for that amount of money, Haddok must be dead at least fifty times by now."

"I don't reckon so. The word I hear is that Haddok is said to be so good with a six gun there ain't been a rush of takers."

"You say Beecham is in Santa Fe?"

"He must be around there somewhere. There's a man by the name of Malone who is talking for Beecham. He's a gambler at the Empire saloon in Santa Fe."

Partlow began to think about what he had just heard. He had been a while without a job.

Reuben Partlow had been born back in the mountains of eastern Kentucky. His memory of childhood was a blur of bitterness and hatred. Born the third child of strict religious parents, he had been the object of beatings since he could remember. It seemed his daddy had thought he was evil for some reason and was determined to beat him into submission to the Lord. He left there when he was seventeen and had never been back. His final memory of that place was of his mother leaning over the dead body of his daddy, weeping and wailing. Partlow had shot his daddy four times. That stopped the beatings, but the damage had been done. Killing his daddy started a life of killing that had left nearly thirty people dead. It had earned him the name Executioner. The killing and the name had never bothered him. He did it for money. As long as he got paid, it was just a job.

Partlow was a loner. Others knew little about him. Now in his early

17

forties, he had simply gone where people were willing to pay to have somebody killed. The price on Haddok was an opportunity for him. He could make it a long time on twenty thousand dollars.

It did not matter to him that Haddok had a reputation with a six shooter. He was not a gunfighter and had no intention of getting into a shootout. He was a back shooter and ambush killer. He had never owned a pistol. He always scouted his target carefully. In some instances he had spent weeks getting ready for the kill. He would have several ambush sites and shooting positions. Each one would have an easy escape route. When he finally made the kill, he would leave immediately. Most of the time his target never saw him or knew of his presence. No lawman had ever been able to tie him to a killing.

Partlow rolled another cigarette without thinking about what he was doing. His long skinny fingers, stained from the nicotine, produced the cigarette like magic. He lit it and breathed deep. A sense of urgency began to build up within him. He needed to be on his way to Santa Fe. This was one job he couldn't let get away from him.

"Your hoss is ready to go," the blacksmith said, interrupting Partlow's thoughts.

He paid the man and walked his horse outside where he tightened the saddle girth and stepped into the saddle.

The blacksmith watched the unusual man ride off and thought to himself, now that's one strange feller.

Partlow rode into Santa Fe four days later and went straight to the Empire Saloon. He didn't drink whiskey so he just pulled up a chair and rolled himself a smoke. He looked the room over and in no time at all had the man named Malone identified. He waited for his chance and approached Will Malone when he stood up to leave a card game.

Partlow cut him off as he walked toward the bar. "Are you the

Malone who's talking for Beecham and the offer on Haddok's head?"

Malone lowered his voice. "Yes I am. What can I do for you?"

"I'm on my way to Arizona and I wanted to know if the money has been claimed that Beecham promised to whoever kills Haddok."

"Nope! You're still in luck if you plan to collect it." Malone chose not to tell this man  he hadn't had anybody that he knew of even say they were going to try and collect.

"I plan to do just that. You can tell Beecham to get his money ready. I just hope nobody beats me to him."

"Then you had better hurry. That kind of money will bring them from everywhere. Do you mind giving me your name? Beecham will want to know."

"Just tell him the Executioner has signed on for the job."

Malone went a little pale. Standing before him was one of the most talked about killers known to man. Just looking at him made Malone feel uneasy. The man's cold eyes and distant look sent a chill through his body. Then the thought came to him, I can't wait to tell Beecham.

Without saying anything further, Partlow turned and walked out. Malone followed him to the door to see him already mounted and riding down the street. Malone felt good. He had a taker.

19

## Southern New Mexico

Filipe Mendoza was the most notorious outlaw along the Mexican border. He headed a gang that numbered in the twenties. They raided back and forth on both sides of the border and had hideouts scattered around in five different places. Mendoza was a ruthless man who had no finesse about his life. He and his men pillaged the country, taking what hey wanted. He always left dead people in his path. He didn't mind killing men, women, or children. Most of the women who lived through his attacks usually wished they had been killed. He reveled in his reputation and the fear he caused.

They were currently in a hideout on the United States side of the border. It was in a secluded mountain canyon that only had one access. It was through a narrow winding pass that would only accommodate one horse at a time at certain places. When they were in this hideout, they always kept a guard stationed at the pass to sound a warning or hold off any approaching enemy. One man could do that easily.

It was early evening and the mountain air was cool. Mendoza and his men were seated around their campfires. They had been in New Mexico for two days and were waiting the return of one of their gang who had gone to scout out their next target. It was a small settlement about fifteen miles away. They were in need of supplies and money. Mendoza had sent Shake Howard to check the place out and make sure they would not be riding into any organized resistence. Some of the small settlements had developed plans to defend themselves and Mendoza had recognized that he had better be a little more careful.

Shake Howard was one of six gringos in the gang. He was a wanted man with a string of killings to his credit. Mendoza had sent him because he had a disarming manner that would allow him to walk around and talk to people without raising suspicion.

The discussion of the moment was focused on the fact that it was past time for Howard to return.

"Shake must have found some trouble," Mendoza said.

"There's not much trouble Shake can't handle," a lanky gringo named Potts replied. "More than likely he found a woman."

The outlaws laughed but their laughter was interrupted by Mendoza. "He better not be laid up with a woman while we are out here eating this dust."

The crowd quieted down and returned to their own worlds around the campfire. The life of an outlaw was boring when there was no action. Hiding out and not attracting attention led to a special kind of boredom that they were all experiencing right now. A few bottles of whiskey would have helped.

It was well after dark when a single round of rifle fire broke the silence. The men quickly moved away from the fires and prepared for trouble. They knew someone was coming through the pass and they figured it to be Shake Howard. When Howard rode up to the fires, they all walked back out and sat down to hear his report.

"Well, boss, the little town is quiet as a prairie. It will be easy pickings. There ain't enough guns in the place to cause us any trouble," Howard spoke in his slow drawl.

"What took you so long, amigo?" Mendoza asked.

"Getting the information you wanted didn't take long at all,"

21

Howard added. "What I found out while hanging around the saloon did take a while."

"What did you hear that was so interesting?" Mendoza asked.

"There's a man in Santa Fe that has placed a big bounty on the head of another man out in Arizona. The amount is twenty thousand dollars and it goes to whoever kills the man. The one who's paying is named Loyd Beecham. He's doing his talking through a gambler named Will Malone at the Empire Saloon in Santa Fe. The feller he wants killed is named Haddok and he lives somewhere near Prescott in the Arizona Territory."

Every man around the fire sucked air when they heard the twenty thousand dollars. Howard continued. "It was all the people in the saloon wanted to talk about. I acted like I had no interest. I figured you would want me to put all the details together for you so I forced myself to set there and drink a little more whiskey." Howard laughed.

"How many men does Haddok have riding with him? "Mendoza asked.

"Nothing was said about that. But I figured that wouldn't make no difference. We could take care of whatever he's got."

"I wonder how many people have taken the man's offer," Mendoza said.

"The talk is there's not been a lot of people headed that way. Some say Haddok is fast with a pistol. Others say he has a name for being tough to handle. I figured he couldn't be as fast as all our guns and twenty thousand is a lot of money."

"Any of you spent time in Santa Fe?" Mendoza asked.

Three of the men said they had. Mendoza settled on one, another gringo named Felton. He told Felton he wanted him to leave at first light and ride to Santa Fe. He was to get word to the gambler that Filipe Mendoza was going to claim the money on Haddok's head.

"Be sure and tell him he better know Haddok is dead before he pays anybody. Tell him I will bring Haddok's body to Santa Fe."

The gang began to talk among themselves and it was obvious Shake Howard had brought them the best news they had heard in a long time.

Mendoza stood up. "We'll leave at first light as well, and head for the settlement Howard scouted for us and take everything we need for the ride to Arizona. Cortez, you will stay here and guard the camp. Felton will return here from Santa Fe and help you. Now get some sleep and be ready to ride at sunup."

Four days later Will Malone was on his way to the general store in Santa Fe when he was stopped by a man on the street. He had never seen the man before.

"Are you the man that is handling the bounty on Haddok's head?" the man asked.

"I'm the man," Malone answered.

"I've been sent here to tell you that Filipe Mendoza and his men are on their way to Arizona to kill Haddok. He told me to tell you not to pay that money until you know Haddok is dead. He said he would bring you his body."

"I know of your boss. I'm proud he's on his way," Malone answered. "And believe me, the man who is paying will look forward to seeing Haddok's body."

Felton turned and Malone watched him ride out. Things are looking up, Malone thought. First the executioner and now Felipe Mendoza. Haddok don't have long to live.

## *Santa Fe*

**R**aven Stull sat on her bed, a small brown bottle cradled in her hands. She had come to this point countless times before. Memories of better times always flooded her mind when she held it. She thought of her mama and daddy and the love and security they had given her. If she only had them now, she thought.

Raven was a saloon girl. She had never wanted to be one and she couldn't stand the thought that she would always be one. She rubbed the smooth contours of the bottle, the liquid barely visible inside the darkened glass. It would be so simple. It wouldn't hurt and it would soon be over. She thought back to one of the times when her mother gave her the bottle..

It had been a normal day. Raven and her family had lived on the homestead farm in northern New Mexico since she was two. She had just turned twelve. Her daddy and brother were working outside and she was helping her mama cook dinner.

She heard the Indians scream and the sound of gunfire. Her mama grabbed her by the arm and pushed her through a trap door in the kitchen floor to the root cellar. They had rehearsed this many times and actually had done it two times before during Indian attacks. Her mother handed her the bottle.

"You know what to do," her mama had said.

Indeed she knew. Her mama had told her earlier, while preparing for a time like this. "Don't open this bottle unless the Indians begin tearing open the door to the cellar. If they do, then open it and drink it as quick as

24

you can. It want hurt none and it will soon be all over. It'll keep you from suffering through what they would do to you."

She didn't have to use it that day. She hid in the cellar until it became quiet, lingering on in there for hours. She knew her folks were dead. If not, they would have already come to get her out. She sobbed quietly and settled on the fact that she was all alone. After a while she mustered the strength to face what was outside. Opening the cellar door, she climbed out to find the mutilated bodies of her mama, daddy, and brother. The darkness hid most of the carnage. She could not see them clearly and she dared not light a lantern. She felt each one and sobbed as the coolness of their bodies welcomed her touch.

She walked away into the night in the direction she thought their nearest neighbors lived. Her family had visited with them in the past, but she had never made the trip at night, and alone. When she staggered into the Beasley's yard the next morning, they took her in and listened to her story. Mrs. Beasley let her sleep while Mr. Beasley went and buried her folks.

Living with them was a miserable existence. They already had four kids and they could hardly get by before she came. She worked hard to make them think she was carrying her load. She had nowhere else to go. By the time she was sixteen she felt almost like a slave to them. She did everything no one else wanted to do. She could handle that. It was when old man Beasley started trying to get her alone with him that she made up her mind to leave.

A family came through heading west in a wagon and she saw her chance. She hid out down the road and when they passed by she begged a ride. She told them she needed to leave. They seemed to understand. She traveled with them as far as Santa Fe.

She found a job her first day there. She mopped and cleaned floors

25

along with other chores at the Empire Saloon. It didn't pay much, but it gave her a place to eat and sleep. It was not long before everybody was carrying on about how pretty she was and they started letting her wait on tables. She was now twenty years old and the prettiest of the fourteen women who worked at the Empire. Her long brown hair and beautiful figure were the first things the men looked for when they came in.

She had heard her boss say you needed four things to have a good saloon: good whiskey, gambling, music, and pretty women. The Empire could hold its own with every saloon in Santa Fe, especially when it came to women. Raven was the only one of the fourteen who had not become the property of some man. She was determined she would amount to something. If she lost her sense of decency, it would all be lost. The rest of the women thought she was crazy.

And on this particular day, sitting on the bed, she almost felt that way too. She couldn't bear the thought of never being able to escape the life that she had fallen into. But now, just like all the other times, she only rubbed the bottle one last time and placed it in the drawer by her bed. Then she stood up and looked in the mirror, touching her hair to make sure it was in place. She walked out the door and down the stairs into the music and laughter she knew so well.

As she waited on the men around the tables, conversations were centered on the price that had been placed on Haddok's head. One of the men yelled across the room to Will Malone and laughed as he said it, "Is Haddok dead yet?"

Malone was agitated by the question and did not respond, but the entire saloon erupted in laughter. Haddok had been all the talk since the news of a twenty thousand bounty had spread. Malone had secretly wished that his name had not been associated with the offer. It made him very uneasy. It also bothered him that Haddok had become something of a folk hero. People were actually laying bets on the outcome. The majority were betting on Haddok. Malone knew that if Haddok survived, he would have to run for his life. Haddok had to die.

Malone left the table and walked to the bar. Raven followed him. "Tell me what you know about Haddok. Is he an awful person?"

"Why are you interested in Haddok?" Malone asked.

"I've just been thinking. I might know someone who could kill him. I don't think this person could kill him unless he is the kind of person who needs killing."

"I don't know much except he has hurt and killed a lot of people."

Raven's mind drifted. I've got to get out of this saloon. I've never hurt a person in my life. I have no way out. I will never become like the rest of the women. Could I kill Haddok if I had the chance?

Malone interrupted her thinking. "Who do you know that might kill Haddok?"

"If I was a man, I might try it myself. That twenty thousand dollars could be my ticket out of this saloon."

"You might have a better chance claiming the money as a woman. Most of the men don't want any part of it."

Raven immediately thought about her bottle of poison. It would be simple and easy if she could get close enough. Twenty thousand dollars was enough for her to start over. She asked Malone, "Would Beecham really pay me if I killed Haddok?"

"Sure! He wants him dead."

"Then I think I'll go to Prescott and give it a try. This could be my only chance in a lifetime."

"Listen, Raven. You kill him and I'll see you get the money."

Raven immediately bought a stage ticket and left the next day for

27

Arizona. Will Malone was the only person who knew where she was going and why.

Malone thought to himself, the offer has been on the table for nearly a month and I have only three takers that I know of, and one of them is a woman. I thought that twenty thousand dollars would have made the crowd of killers going to Prescott look like a cattle stampede. I'd better keep the back door open so I can get out of here in a hurry if I need to.

*Prescott*

It had been quiet in Prescott for over a month. The townsfolk were enjoying the peace. It was into this calm that a storm came calling. It was noon on a Tuesday. There was a pretty good crowd in the Eagle Saloon. The good times were back again and the music and laughter seemed more like a Saturday night than the middle of the day on Tuesday.

The stranger walked through the swinging doors and made his way to the bar. After ordering a drink, he turned to case the crowd. The bartender slid his drink over to him and asked, "Where you from, pardner?"

"I'm from back east and I'm heading west to try a little of that digging for gold. I figure it would be a lot easier than punching cows."

The stranger and the bartender talked on while the bartender worked. He enjoyed the news from back east and it was always good to talk to somebody different from the everyday crowd. It was during this private conversation that the bartender jumped back a bit and hollered for everybody in the place to listen.

"Hey, fellers! This gent is from back east and he just rode in toting some news you all would probably want to hear. Tell'em what you just told me."

"I told him you folks better be getting ready for the crowd. There's a man named Beecham back in Santa Fe that has put a twenty thousand dollar bounty on the head of one of your crowd here in Prescott. The money goes to whoever kills a man by the name of Haddok."

29

Every person in the saloon gathered around the stranger and began drilling him. He told them that he didn't know much. What he did know, he had heard in a small town on his way west.

"I heard there's a gambler by the name of Malone who is handling the deal for Beecham. Malone hangs out at the Empire Saloon in Santa Fe. Why, I figured this place would be covered up with people trying to claim that money."

One man responded, "We all know Beecham and it sounds like something he would do. The way he left out of here, none of us figured he'd come back hisself." They all laughed. "I can tell you one thing, feller. Whoever comes has got his work cut out for him. Anybody who knows Reed Haddok would tell you that twenty thousand ain't near enough." They all laughed again.

While they continued to talk about this turn of events, a man by the name of Folsom left the saloon and hurried down to the sheriff's office. Sheriff Burgess listened with shock as Folsom told him the news.

The sheriff then left his office and saddled up. He had to get word to Haddok. He rode out of town toward the Rocking H at a steady clip. He hardly noticed the young man he passed as he rode out.

Red Cheatham was barely eighteen. He wore two tied down pistols. Everybody in his hometown of Axle told him he was the fastest man with the draw they had ever seen. Axle was small, but that didn't matter. Red knew he was good. He had never been in a gunfight. He practiced all the time and he was a good shot. All he needed was someone to stand up to him. When he heard the offer on Haddok's head, he knew who the first man would be to die at his hands. He rode cockily into Prescott with the dream of twenty thousand dollars dancing in his head. He had nodded at the man with the badge when they passed but the sheriff acted like he hadn't seen him. It didn't matter none though. Sheriff or no sheriff, there was going to be a killing in Prescott.

Sheriff Burgess made it to the Rocking H by late afternoon. He found Reed Haddok with his cowhands in the middle of branding. When he rode up Haddok and Josh Spencer walked over to shake hands and exchange pleasantries.

The sheriff said, "Reed, I need to talk to you privately."

Spencer replied, "Don't keep him too long Sheriff. He lets me do all the work anyway." He grinned and walked away.

"What you got on your mind, Sheriff. You didn't ride all the way out here just to get to see me I know." Haddok spoke with a smile. These men were friends.

"I've got some bad news. Beecham seems to have made it to Santa Fe. We got word in town today that he's put a twenty thousand dollar bounty on your head. The money goes to whoever kills you. A man by the name of Will Malone, a gambler, is handling this for Beecham. Malone hangs out at the Empire Saloon in Santa Fe. I rode out as soon as I heard it because there's no telling when people will start showing up trying to collect that money."

Haddok mulled over the news for a minute as he looked at the disappointment in the sheriff's eyes. He knew the sheriff wanted to help, but like a lot of things in life, there ain't nobody that can take your troubles away. You just have to face them. "I appreciate you coming out to warn me," Haddok responded. "I guess I should have killed Beecham. You can count on one thing. He's had his chance to live."

"I'll try to head off anything I can, Reed," the sheriff added. "But there's just so much I can do to help you."

"I know. I don't expect you to get in this, Sheriff. I would appreciate it if you don't say anything to the men. I want to tell them myself."

31

The sheriff agreed and they said their farewells. Reed watched as he rode off and thought, well, hell is coming for a visit. I guess I'd better get ready to welcome him.

Haddok returned to the work at hand and did not mention what the sheriff had told him. He would choose his time to tell the others.

As he worked through the remainder of the afternoon, he began to think about his situation. He had thought the manner in which he had humiliated Loyd Beecham would be the end of his concern with him. It seems he was wrong and an angry man was now bent on revenge. Haddok knew that twenty thousand dollars was enough money to cause a lot of people to come looking for him. His problem was, he didn't know who, how, or when. This would require him to change his pattern of activity and to live his life on constant alert. His first step would be to tell the people close around him and give them the chance to leave. He did not want people being hurt on account of him. His second step would be to ride to the Diamond and tell Samantha and her father. His thinking was already focusing on their need to maintain a distance from him. He surely didn't want them to get hurt in this.

They wrapped up their work for the day and rode back to the ranch. Haddok decided to tell them while they were all gathered for supper. The place was buzzing with loud talk and laughter as the men sat around the tables in the bunkhouse. Josh and Reed had taken to eating with the cowhands so it was not unusual for them both to be present. The talking died down as the men ate and they were about finished when Haddok stood up.

"I have something to say to you men that will affect all of you," Haddok said. "Listen to me for a minute."

They all stopped what they were doing and turned to give him their attention.

32

"Sheriff Burgess rode out this afternoon and brought me some news I think you need to know about. It seems Loyd Beecham has put a twenty thousand dollar bounty on my head, payable to whoever kills me." He looked them in the eyes for a moment and flashed his smile as he continued. "Now that's an awful lot of money. I hope none of you decide you want to get rich quick."

They all laughed and started to express their feelings when he stopped them.

"I know there will be people who will act on his offer. I want you to know that I don't expect you to stay here and put your life on the line. This is a personal thing with me and I'll have no hard feelings toward you if you ride out. This ranch will be a target for a spell. If you stay on, I don't expect you to do my fighting. The trouble is, they may not give you a choice."

Once again the men tried to express themselves but Haddok cut them off short.

"Josh did not know about this until now. What I'm saying to you goes for him too. I'm going to leave and let you talk about it. Just know that I appreciate what you've done to get this place back into shape. Josh can pay your wages if you want to leave. You will have my respect if you do."

That said, Haddok walked out and headed straight to the house. The place was in a roar as he left. Only a few minutes had passed when Josh walked in and delivered the message.

"Reed, to a man they say they ride for the brand. They believe in you and they will fight with you." Josh gave him that look that the two had learned to exchange, and then said, "They had to pressure me, but I guess I'll hang around with them."

"You don't know how good that makes me feel. You're going to have to help me take care of these men. They don't know what they're up against. I want you to start thinking about defending the ranch. I'm heading out for the Diamond in the morning. I've got to talk to Mr. Forbes and Samantha. I don't want them too close to this thing. They could get hurt."

They talked a while longer and then turned in. Reed went to sleep with a chair against the door and his pistol on his chest. It had been a spell since he had done that.

*Santa Fe . . .*

A horrible scream broke the silence. Beecham's body was tightly drawn into a ball, his arms raised to protect his face. Both body and bed were drenched. He was shaking uncontrollably.

This was the worst one yet. It seemed the nightmares had become more intense each time. They did not come every night, but they were getting more frequent. While not exactly alike, they were enough alike to seem like repetitions of the same event.

Tonight's fearful moment had seeped from the depths of some rambling dream. He had answered a knock at the door. Haddok was there. It was like death standing there smiling. Haddok reached for him and he screamed, waking himself. Anyone who knew Beecham would never have thought he would look like he did at the moment. He was a whimpering, broken, and frightened man.

After the fact registered that this was just another dream, Beecham began to calm down. He lit a lamp and poured himself a drink. He thought to himself, I hope no one ever knows the depth of the fear Haddok has brought into my life.

As each day passed without hearing a word about Haddok's death, Beecham became more aware that he could show up at any time. Just the thought of being confronted fueled his fear. He knew what he had to do. As soon as it was daylight, he would get word to Malone to meet him. He had to risk a meeting because he didn't want to have his instructions in writing.

Malone arrived at Beecham's house early in the morning. Beecham

35

was finished with breakfast and was drinking a last cup of coffee when Roseta showed him in.

"Have a chair, Will," Beecham said. "Want a cup of coffee?"

"Thanks. I could use one," Malone responded.

Roseta left and returned with a steaming cup for Malone. After she left, Beecham began to share his plans.

"I'm going to be leaving soon. I'm getting ready to return to Prescott and claim my property. I have a place in mind to hole up closer to Prescott. I'm heading there to begin rounding up a bunch of gunhands. We'll be ready to ride as soon as we hear about Haddok's death. I want you to send a rider to alert me just as soon as you get the word."

"I don't like it," Malone came back. "You're leaving me here to face Haddok if your scheme don't work. He'll show here and I'll be trapped. I've been thinking a lot about that lately and I don't mind telling you I feel like I'm being set up," Malone said.

"Will, I'm paying you a lot of money to work for me. If you want to ride out, then do it. But don't you ever try to come back to me after you leave," Beecham said.

"I know you've been good to me. It just makes me a little edgy to feel like you've put me out front with a man that has scared you enough to run you into a hole."

"I'm not leaving because I'm scared," Beecham responded. "Haddok is as good as dead and you know it. I'm just getting ready to move in when I hear the word."

"What do you want me to do?" Malone asked.

"When you know he's dead, send a rider to the stage office at Fort Defiance. Seal me a message in a letter and put Frank Lain's name on the outside. I'll send somebody there every few days to check. As soon as I get the word, you'll be able to get a hold of me in Prescott," Beecham said.

36

"What if I don't hear anything?"

"Then I'll just have to come up with another way of having him killed," Beecham replied.

They talked a while and Malone left. As he walked down the hill toward his hotel, he thought over his situation. He grew a little nervous as he thought. I've been out here on this limb by myself for a while now. I ought to saddle up and ride. But like all the other times in his life, the right decision seemed to escape him.

Beecham went to the bank as soon as it opened and did everything necessary to take care of his financial needs for the next few months. With a sack full of cash and letters of credit in hand, he bought a ticket west on the stage and left the next day.

As the stage pulled out of Santa Fe, he thought, maybe I'll be able to sleep tonight. Haddok would visit him again that night. It would be the worst one yet.

*Eastern New Mexico near the Texas border*

Smoke filled the room and somehow seemed to amplify the small talk that made it hard for a man to hear. Nobody seemed to notice the stranger who pushed away from his table and walked out the door. Doc had been in this small and out of the way settlement just south of Fort Sumner for only about an hour.

Doc was on his way home to Texas. His trip to Arizona had been to clean up a town by the name of Prescott. When he got there, he found his son had already done that. He also learned that Reed had become owner of a ranch along with Josh Spencer.

Doc had hidden the fact that he was a hired gun from his children. Their knowledge of him was that he was a wandering man. His trip back to Texas was filled with pride and concern. He was so proud of his son. Yet, his encounter with the gunslinger Ike Craven and the knowledge that Loyd Beecham had hired Craven to kill his son caused him worry. He had been fortunate to bump into Craven and killing him was an unavoidable circumstance. He had wondered if killing Craven would stop Beecham. He had just gotten his answer.

When he rode into the small settlement, he had hoped for a bath, meal, and a place to sleep. He had opted for the meal first and was just digging into a steak and a pot of coffee when he overheard the men talking at the next table.

"Have you heard about the price they have on the head of that Texas boy out in Arizona?" one man asked.

"Nope," another shrugged. "What about it?"

"There's a man in Santa Fe by the name of Beecham who has put a twenty thousand dollars bounty on the head of a young feller from Texas. His name is Haddok and he hails from the Brazos River country. Haddok is living out around Prescott. The word is Haddok is one tough man. For some reason Beecham wants Haddok dead and is willing to pay whoever kills him," the first man answered.

"Who is Beecham?" another asked.

"Well, the way I heard it, no one seems to know Beecham. He's making his offer through a gambler named Will Malone. Malone hangs around the Empire saloon in Santa Fe," the talkative gent continued.

Doc, without attracting attention, paid up and pushed away from his steak. When he left he went straight out and saddled up. He muttered to his horse, "Well boy, we are almost in Texas, but it looks like we're going to have to take a little side trip." He wrote the names of Beecham and Malone, along with the Empire Saloon, on his brain. It would take him a few days to get to Santa Fe. However, it would be worth the trip to look into the eyes of the men who were trying to kill his son.

He rode into Santa Fe late in the day five days later. He put his horse up at a livery and rented a room in the Barton Hotel. It was one of three that lined the main street. He had time to visit a general merchandise store and buy some new trousers, a shirt, and a long black coat. Upon returning to the hotel, he caught a bath, changed into his new clothes, had a good meal, and then walked across the street to the Empire Saloon. He had chosen the hotel and the street front room because it gave him a good view of the saloon.

When he walked into the saloon he gave no indication, by his looks or demeanor, of the serious nature of his mission. He wore no visible gun, but he had a pistol tucked snugly in his belt beneath the long coat.

His entrance had gone unnoticed. He walked to the bar and ordered a drink. He was not a drinking man, but having one before him was important to his ruse. He wanted to fit in.

A casual glance revealed four card games in progress and a large crowd sitting at tables drinking and talking. The bar was fairly lined with men. The working women were busy selling whiskey and flirting.

He had no idea what Will Malone looked like and his immediate goal was to identify him. He stood at the bar, seemingly in his own world, for the best part of an hour. He had intentionally spilled some of his drink and then a little later he switched glasses and eased his down the bar. He ordered another from the bartender. He spotted an empty table to one side and walked over to take a seat. He was not there long when one of the ladies approached.

"Can I get you anything else, big fellow?" she asked, flashing her smile and batting long eyelashes.

"I'm okay for now," Doc responded. "It seems like they're keeping you busy tonight."

"No. This is about a normal night. Are you new in town?"

"I live a little north of here and came down on some business. I'm going to be in town a few days. I like to gamble a little. Are the poker games always open?"

"Oh yes. We've got a bunch of men who come every night and play poker. The high stakes game is the table in the far corner," she said.

"Thanks," Doc responded. "I might amble over that way and watch for a while."

"Help yourself," she tossed over her shoulder as she walked away. "My name is Linda. If you need anything, just yell."

"Sure thing," Doc replied. He sat there a while and then walked over near the high stakes game. He felt this to be his best bet to put a face on Will

Malone. The players glanced at him but quickly lost themselves back in the game.

There were five men at the table and two wore clothes that marked them as professionals. One was thin and looked to be in his sixties. The other was well built and Haddok guessed him to be about forty.

He watched for a few minutes, then walked back to the bar. He placed his glass on the top and turned to leave. He drew up short when he heard a man shout across the room.

"Hey, Malone! What about Haddok? Has anybody collected the money on his head yet?"

Doc turned toward the high stakes table. The younger of the two he had pegged as professional gamblers spouted out a string of cuss words that was quickly followed by an uproar of laughter throughout the saloon. Doc smiled and walked out. He now had a face to put with the name.

He headed back to the hotel, went to his room, and pulled a chair over by the window. Taking a seat in the dark room, he thought, I'll just wait and see where he heads when he leaves.

He could see the poker game Malone was in through the saloon window. Malone was facing the window. Doc fetched his eyeglass and steadied it on his knee. He studied the man's face. It was hard and punctuated by a thin mustache.

It was well after midnight when the game broke up. Doc watched the people leave and spotted Malone as he walked out the door. To his surprise, Malone walked straight across the street as if he was heading for the very hotel Doc was in. He thought, could I be so lucky?

Doc walked quickly across the dark room and opened his door a crack. He heard someone climbing the stairs and saw a shadow pass his door. He widened the crack a bit and watched as Malone entered a room

41

about halfway down the hall. He made a mental note of the distance and quietly closed the door.

He knew how to find Will Malone. Now he had to find Loyd Beecham.

Doc was up early and after breakfast he made his way onto the streets. He had three places he wanted to visit during the day. The first was the bank.

The Cattleman's Bank opened for business at nine o'clock. Doc walked in a few minutes later. He asked to speak to the owner and was ushered into an office and introduced to a short chubby man by the name of Otis Barnwell.

"Hello Mr. Barnwell. My name is Grant Hipps," Doc said as he extended his hand.

They shook hands and exchanged pleasantries.

"I'm in town on business and I'm going to be moving a part of my business to Santa Fe," Doc continued.

"That's wonderful," Barnwell replied. "We'd be proud to offer you our services."

"I'm in the cattle business. I'm going to be bringing a lot of them here for sale and shipment. I'll need a good bank and you've come highly recommended," Doc said casually.

"Great. Who gave us the recommendation?"

"A man by the name of Loyd Beecham. I met him on a trip to Arizona and when he learned I was going to shift my business to Santa Fe, he told me about your bank." Doc noticed a puzzled look on Barnwell's face and for a moment there was silence.

"I hate to tell you this, but I don't even know Loyd Beecham. His name has been connected to Santa Fe in a way I'm not proud of. None of us who have been here a while can recall ever meeting him," Barnwell said.

"That sure is strange," Doc came back. "He spoke as if this was his home territory. Maybe I just misunderstood him."

"Well, we'd be proud to have your business. However, I wish I could put a tag on Beecham. There's a lot of us who would like to meet him."

"You'll get my business," Doc replied. "I'll be in town a few days. Before I leave, I'll come by and take care of the paperwork and open an account."

They both expressed their farewells. Doc walked out and headed for the sheriff's office. It was down the street from the bank and Doc entered to meet Gus Wilkerson, chief lawman of Santa Fe. They exchanged handshakes and Wilkerson offered Doc a seat.

Doc began. "I'm Grant Hipps and I am in town on business. I thought it would be good if we met."

"Good to meet you, Grant. What kind of business are you in?"

"I am in the cattle business up north and I am going to start bringing my cattle here for sale and shipment," Doc answered. "I will not always be with my men when they come down so I wanted to meet you and let you know that if you ever have any problems with my outfit, I'll stand with you in correcting things."

"Well, that's great. I wish more folks were like you."

Doc let a little frown run across his face, and then continued, "I must say that one of the factors that helped me make up my mind to come here was the reputation that this was a law abiding town. However, when I told the banker, a Mr. Barnwell, the name of the man who recommended his bank to me, Barnwell seemed a little disturbed. He didn't even know the man and indicated the man's reputation might not be all that good."

"Who was the man?" the sheriff asked.

"He told me he was Loyd Beecham. I met him out west of here and he talked like he was a regular in Santa Fe," Doc said.

The sheriff seemed a little disturbed when he heard the name and replied, "Beecham's name has been like a buzzing bee around here, but nobody knows him. The talk of this town for weeks has been connected to Beecham. The story is being passed around that he has put a price, a big price, on the head of a man by the name of Haddok out in the Arizona territory. It seems his offer is good for whoever kills Haddok. Supposedly, his contact person for Santa Fe is a gambler named Will Malone. Now I don't like Malone and I would run him out of town if I had a reason. He's broken no law on my books that I know of. I've kept my eye on him to see if he would lead me to Beecham, but so far he hasn't. So, you see, when you mentioned Beecham to Barnwell, he naturally reacted. None of us around here appreciate that kind of reputation. Tell me where you met Beecham and what he looks like."

Doc made up an encounter and description. Then he said, "This all is very strange. Yet, it does not affect my business at all." Their conversation left the subject of Beecham and soon ended in another shake of hands. Doc left and looked up and down the street until his eyes settled on the third place he had planned to visit. It was time for a haircut and shave.

The barber's name was Slick McVay. Doc chuckled to himself when McVay welcomed him. He wondered why most barbers he had known were bald headed. Slick had a man in the chair and two others were waiting. Doc took a seat and answered a few of the questions the men asked of all newcomers. Comfortable with the fact that Doc was a cattleman in town on business, they soon returned to barbershop talk. After a while, the conversation turned to the subject Doc had an interest in. He listened to the men talk about the hiring of killers. It was obvious that the matter did not set well with them. Doc remained silent and waited his turn in the barber's chair. When he finally took his seat, the other men had left. Doc seized the opportunity.

"McVay, have you ever met Loyd Beecham?" Doc asked.

"You can call me Slick. Everybody else does. To answer your question, nope. Neither has anybody else in Santa Fe, unless it's that Malone feller."

Doc continued, "Slick, I'm going to take you into my confidence. It's real important you not tell anybody what I'm about to tell you. Can you do that?"

"Sure I can," Slick replied. "If I told everything I know about people in this town, there would be quite a stir."

"I'm pretty good at sizing people up, and I had you pegged as the kind of man you could trust."

Slick kind of beamed when Doc said that.

"But you remember, what I'm going to tell you could get you killed," Doc added.

Slick's look became a little more serious.

Doc talked on, "I'm a special law enforcement agent and I've been on Beecham's trail for a spell. When I learned about the offer to pay someone to kill Haddok coming out of Santa Fe, I made a fast trip here."

Slick was taking all this in with genuine interest. Doc felt sure he was buying his story.

Doc continued, "The way I have it figured out, if Beecham came to Santa Fe, it would have been about three months back, give or take a little. I hear Haddok had fairly beaten his face to a pulp. Since Beecham is not going by his real name and you probably shave and cut the hair of most men in town, I was wondering if you recollect anybody coming in who appeared to have been in a fight? Oh; there's one other thing. Beecham has a lot of money."

46

Slick thought for a minute. "I would never have thought nothing about it if you hadn't jogged my brain. A little over two months ago I had a man come in who had some fresh scars and the remains of some scabs on his face. He's a well thought of man in these parts. His name is Frank Lain. He's been gone out west on some business for over a year. He was a regular here before then. He always pays me more than I charge and he's a likable feller. However, he fits all three of the things you talked about."

"Where does he live?" Doc asked.

"It's funny, but he was in here last week and said he was going to be gone for another spell," Slick added. "He lives at the top of the hill behind the main street. It's a big adobe house with a fence around it."

Doc thanked him and again reminded him to tell nobody about their conversation. If all went well, he didn't care who he talked to tomorrow. He paid for his haircut, shook Slick's hand, and walked out on the street. He found the road that went up to the high ground and headed that way.

As he made his way up the hill that was covered with houses, his mind went back over what he had learned. Beecham was not a man known to the people of Santa Fe. If Frank Lain was in fact Beecham, then he had a little better understanding of how the plan to kill his son was being carried out. Beecham was obviously a smart man. If he had left Santa Fe, then Will Malone was perhaps his only link to finding him.

Doc located the house belonging to Frank Lain easily and was just opening the gate to the yard when a Mexican man came out the front door and spoke from the porch.

"Can I help you, Senor?" the man asked.

"I'm looking for Frank Lain," Doc said. "I met him out west a few weeks back and he invited me to visit him when I came through Santa Fe. Is he home?"

"No, he is not. He left last week on a business trip out west."

"Well, when he returns, tell him that Grant Hipps was by this way. We hit it off real well out in Arizona and I was hoping to get to see him. I'm leaving town in the morning and I won't be back this way for a spell. Be sure and tell him I came by."

"I will, Senor. I'm sorry he missed you."

"By the way," Doc said as he turned to walk away. "Do you know exactly where he's traveling to?"

"He did not say. He never tells where he is going or when he will be back."

"It doesn't matter," Doc replied. "I just thought I might look him up if our paths crossed." Doc thought for a moment and added, "I was kind of worried about him when he left Arizona. He had gotten into a tussle and got beat up pretty bad."

"Yes, I know Senor. He looked very bad when he returned home. But he is fine now."

Doc thanked the man and walked away from the house and back down the hill. Frank Lain was Loyd Beecham.

**D**oc went straight to the hotel and got his gear together. He then headed for the livery and saddled his horse. He fed him a bait of grain and settled up with the hostler, mounted up, and rode down the street and behind the hotel where he was staying. There was a water trough and hitching post there and he tied his horse up near the trough. Returning to his room, he stretched out on the bed for a nap. He planned on having a busy night.

It was getting on to sundown when he got up and went down to the café for supper. He enjoyed the coffee and a platter of steak and potatoes. He lingered long at the table and had no interest in what was going on around him. His mind had been centered on Will Malone since his walk up the hill. He was anxious to talk to the man who was part of the plot to kill his son. He thought, Malone had best enjoy his card game tonight, because he is going to lose this game of hiring killers before the night is over.

Doc then paid up and walked back to his room. Instead of going in, he eased down the hall and tried the door to Malone's room. It was unlocked so he let it glide open and he looked in. The room was neat and a lamp had been left lit. He closed the door and returned to his room. He took his seat in the dark by the window. He could make out Malone at the poker table down in the saloon. Lying across Doc's bed was his gun belt that also held his knife. He had not been wearing it since he had been in Santa Fe, but he would put it on tonight.

The night wore on and Doc watched as people slowly left the saloon.

49

Malone's card game broke up around midnight and he made his normal trek across the street toward the hotel. Doc belted on his pistol and walked out of the room, down the hall, and into Malone's room. The door opened inward so Doc stood where he would be behind the door when it opened. A few moments later he heard Malone's footsteps. The door knob turned and the door swung open. Malone stepped in and closed the door behind him. His back was to Doc when the arm swung down and the barrel of Doc's pistol struck him in the head. Malone crumpled to the floor. Doc quickly lifted him to the bed where he tied his feet and hands. He stuffed a cloth into his mouth.

Opening the door quietly, Doc took a look up and down the hall. All was clear. He walked back to the bed and picked the man up easily and threw him across his shoulder. Malone made no movement. He was out cold. Doc walked the hall toward the back of the hotel and out a door that led to stairs outside the building. It was a dark night. He stood at the top of the stairs, cradling Malone on his shoulder, looking and listening. Seeing and hearing nothing, he walked down the steps, draped Malone over his saddle, and mounted up behind him. He rode quietly out of town.

He had been riding for a while before Malone started to come around. He had hit him pretty hard and he was hoping he had not killed him before he could find out what he needed to know.

"You better be still and quiet or I'll stop this horse and slit your throat," Doc said.

Malone stiffened and moved no more. Doc rode for about thirty minutes south on a main route out of town and then turned off on a trail by a small stream bed. The stream itself was dry except for an occasional puddle. Doc rode in the stream bed for about a mile and then pulled up in a small scope of trees.

He dismounted and pulled Malone off the horse and let him fall to the ground. Tying his horse, Doc rustled up some sticks and dry limbs to start a fire. He lit it and nursed it until it was burning good. He glanced at Malone from time to time and the man's eyes were a perfect picture of fear.

Doc took his time with the fire and ignored Malone. The fire gave off a warmth that broke the chill and spread enough light for a good look at the man who talked for Loyd Beecham. Doc walked over, pulled Malone up to a sitting position, and jerked the cloth out of his mouth and threw it to the ground. He then walked to the other side of the fire from him and set down. He looked deep into Malone's eyes and spoke, "You better start talking."

"Who are you?" Malone asked.

"I want to hear you tell me the things I need to know," Doc replied.

"I don't know what you want me to say. Who are you? Why have you brought me here like this?"

Doc just stared into Malone's eyes and waited.

"I don't know you and I sure don't know what this is about. If you are going to rob me, then just take what I've got and let me go. I won't tell nobody about this."

Doc remained quiet.

"Look, man! These ropes are killing me. Will you please take the one on my wrists off?" Malone asked.

Doc shook his head. He set there looking at the man and with each passing minute more anxiety spread across Malone's face.

Malone thought to himself, I knew it could come to this. He knew he had been crazy to allow Beecham to put him out in the open. He also knew he should have left town when Beecham did. If this stranger was here as a part of the Haddok thing, then he would just explain to him how he had been made to get involved.

"It's about the price on Haddok's head, ain't it?" Malone quizzed. "Did Haddok send you here?"

Doc said nothing.

Malone continued, "I don't know who you are or who sent you, but I want you to know that this whole thing ain't none of my doing. Beecham hired me a long time back when I was down on my luck and I've always felt like I owed him. I never meant no harm to Haddok or anyone else for that matter."

Doc sat quietly with his hands resting on his lap, his face stoney. Finally, he spoke.

"We have to talk a little bit. If you cooperate, it will be easier for you. If you don't, I'll start with your right ear and I'll cut things off until you are willing."

"I'm willing," Malone spit out. "Would you tell me who you are?"

"The name's Haddok."

It seemed like a sledge hammer had been driven into his gut as Malone answered, "I'll talk."

"I know Loyd Beecham has gone by the name Frank Lain here in Santa Fe," Doc continued. "I also know he has left town. I want to know where he's gone?"

"I don't know," Malone quickly added. "He didn't tell me."

Doc moved so quickly it startled Malone and he fell backwards. Doc knelt over him and grabbed his ear. He slipped his knife out and laid it against the ear, bringing a line of blood when the razor sharp blade touched it.

Malone reacted quickly. "He told me to send a message to the stage office at Fort Defiance in the Arizona territory when I got word that you were dead."

Doc chuckled a bit and said, "It's not me he's trying to kill. It's my son. I'm just doing a little paw work for him. Where is he staying at Fort Defiance and what name is he using?"

52

"I don't know where he's staying. He said he was going to get a bunch of gunfighters together and be ready to go back and claim his holdings in Prescott when he heard that you . . .I mean your son . . .is dead. He told me to send the message addressed to Frank Lain."

"Talk to me straight, Malone. How many people have you sent to kill my son?"

"There ain't been many," Malone answered. "An outlaw gang run by Filipe Mendoza, a back shooter who goes by the name Executioner, and a dance hall girl named Raven Stull are the only ones who have talked to me. Believe me . . .I'm telling you the truth," Malone said.

Doc thought for a minute. "You might as well tell me everything. Beecham has used you as a shield. You should have known that somebody would come looking sooner or later."

"It's the money. Beecham has got plenty of it and it kept me here."

"Well, Malone, you are a gambler. You bought stakes in a game that runs a little too high for your blood. You can believe me on that." Haddok pulled Malone up and cut the rope around his ankles and then the one around his wrists. He pulled the man's coat off his shoulders and down to strip it off over his hands. A pistol was hanging on Malone's hip. Doc spoke, "You've been the lead man in a plot to kill my son. I should have cut your throat while I had you tied. That's exactly what the people you've sent to kill my boy would do. I've never killed a man like that. You hired on in a mighty costly game when you put your chips down on this table. You are fixing to pay. You can draw or you can just stand there. I'm going to kill you. It's a shame you didn't keep better company. When I count to three, I'm drawing."

Malone started to back away protesting, but he heard a calmly spoken "One" and "Two." He clumsily went for his pistol and his hand had barely touched it's handle when he heard the deafening boom of Doc's

53

pistol and was thrown to the ground by the force of the bullet. He never knew when Doc swung into the saddle and rode off into the night.

Four days later Doc walked into a stage office at Fort Sumner near the Texas border. He borrowed some paper and a pencil.

Josh,

Malone is dead. Beecham left Santa Fe. He is using the name
Frank Lain. He is somewhere near Fort Defiance in Arizona.
Seems like only three people have took the job to kill Bud.
An ambusher who goes by the name Executioner, an outlaw
named Mendoza, and a woman named Stull. The outlaw has
a gang with him. Don't know how many. I'm gone to Texas.
Take care of my boy.

Doc

He put the letter in a envelope and wrote Josh Spencer, Prescott, Arizona on the outside and put it in the bag to head west on the next stage. He walked out and mounted up to head for home.

**R**eed Haddok was up early the morning after Sheriff Burgess had brought him the news about the price on his head. After breakfast, he headed out for the Diamond. Josh wanted to ride with him but Reed persuaded him to stay and get the ranch prepared for a possible surprise attack.

He rode with caution and stayed off existing trails, holding to the low ground as much as possible and riding light in the saddle. It was not hard for him to shift into the cautious nature of the hunted. He had no idea who might try to kill him or how. But he knew he would be ready and whoever came would get all of him he wanted. That part came to the surface when anybody brought trouble and it had already moved in before Sheriff Burgess rode out of sight yesterday.

Josh had his plan to defend the ranch in motion. He had talked with Reed about it at breakfast. Half of his men would be stationed at strategic places around the ranch at all times. Two men would be on the high ground immediately behind the ranch. That mountain was the only approach for anyone trying to sneak up on the ranch. Three men would occupy the distant ridge line to the north, east, and south of the ranch house. They would ride to warn them if anyone approached. Three wagons were placed at positions between the ranch buildings. One man would be near the barn, one near the bunkhouse, and one near the house. All the men had been given firing positions in the event of an attack. They had plenty of ammunition for pistols and rifles. Until this danger passed, they would hold these positions in shifts around the clock. If a direct attack was made on the ranch, the attackers would pay a high price. They were ready.

Reed rode into the yard of the Diamond ranch late in the afternoon. He wanted to see Samantha, but now he had to do it with news that was sure to upset her. Sam and her father were both happy to see him and ushered him into the house. Supper was on the table and Sam quickly set an extra plate. Their foreman, Gus Trapp, came in for supper and they all took a seat and dug in. Reed used the time to tell them the news.

"I hoped I had seen the last of Loyd Beecham," Reed said. "Sheriff Burgess rode out to tell me he had heard that Beecham had put a twenty thousand dollar bounty on my head."

They were all three shocked.

"I wanted you folks to know about it for a couple of reasons. First, I want you to keep your distance from the Rocking H. There is no need for you to be drawn into this. Second, I wanted you to know, Samantha, because I don't know that I can be talking to you on a regular basis for a spell."

"Now wait a minute," Forbes blurted out. "Your trouble is our trouble. There is no way we are going to back off."

"I know I can count on you to help if I need you. I just don't know what to expect. I think I can handle it better if I'm not worried about the two of you." Reed looked over at Sam, hoping she would understand.

"Now listen, Reed," Sam said. "You have helped us through some tough times at the risk of your life. Please don't ask us to stay away."

"The truth is, Sam, I don't want you to stay away. But I can handle it much better if I'm not worried about you."

They talked on through the meal and continued on the porch until late. Forbes and Gus then said goodnight and left the couple alone.

"Reed, is it always going to be like this? Will you ever know any peace?" Sam asked.

"I hope so. I didn't plan for this to happen."

"I wish you had killed Beecham when you had the chance."

"I probably should have. But I didn't have to then. I guess I'll have to the next time around."

"I don't understand you, Reed Haddok," Sam said, agitation in her voice. "If you think I'm going to spend my life wondering whether or not you are dead or alive, you are crazy."

Reed suddenly stood up, mounted his horse, and rode off into the dark with Sam's voice calling him back.

Sam sat on the porch and cried into the morning hours. She had never felt such pain. She was in love. She knew she had acted like a child, but she couldn't help it.

Reed rolled into his blanket about two miles from the Diamond and tried to sleep. Sam's words would not go away. He could not blame her. It was just that he had never felt this way before. He didn't know what to say or do. Leaving was the only thing he knew to do. Maybe I should have stayed, he thought. He looked at the sky and fought the urge to get up and ride back to the Diamond. Unable to sleep, he rolled up his gear, saddled up, and headed for Prescott.

Filipe Mendoza and his gang, twenty two strong, had ridden into Prescott at about the same time Reed Haddok had been having supper with his friends at the Diamond ranch. In a strange mixture of timing, Mendoza had been the last of the three who had signed on to kill Haddok to show up in Prescott.

Rubin Partlow arrived there two days earlier. His only contact with the townspeople had been at the general store where he loaded up with supplies and tobacco. He also stopped by the blacksmith shop to have more work done on a shoe that kept working loose on his horse.      Raven Stull had come in on the stage three days back. She was staying in a room at the boarding house above the café at Fort Misery. She had been quietly meeting people and inquiring about Haddok's ranch.

ᕦ ᕦ ᕦ ᕦ

Mendoza and his men tied up in front of the Eagle Saloon and went in to unwind. Their arrival caused a stir and most of the townspeople headed home early just to get off the street. It is not often that you have that many gunhands drinking it up at one time. The local folk could recognize trouble when they saw it and this bunch sure had the look.

The gang began to wash the trail dust down their throats and pair off with the women. Mendoza himself wanted information.

"Where is the Rocking H ranch from here?" he asked the bartender.

58

"About twenty miles or so northeast," he replied. "The main road out of town in that direction splits after about a mile. You take the left one and follow it. You can't miss the wagon ruts. You have business at the Rocking H?"

"I want to find the man they call Haddok. Do you know him?"

"Everybody around here knows him. Why are you looking for him?"

Mendoza laughed. "We just have a little business with him." He then walked over to where a few of his men were seated around a table. He took a chair and shared what he had learned. He never noticed the older man as he left the saloon, heading straight for the sheriff's office. Burgess was busy at his desk and looked up when he heard the door open.

"What's going on Fred? It's kinda late in the day for you to be in town, ain't it?"

"I had dropped some firewood off at the general store and was getting me a drink at the Eagle before going home. We just had a passle of what looks to be gunslingers ride in. They're all down at the saloon. Must be at least twenty of them. They're asking questions about Haddok. I just thought you would want to know."

"Thanks for telling me Fred. Now you run on home," the sheriff replied.

After Fred left, the sheriff eased out onto the street and made his way up to the Eagle. He looked in the window and realized he was facing a situation that could easily get him killed. He walked back to his office and thought it over.

A little later, he walked down to the café and looked inside to see a ranch hand from one of the spreads around Prescott. He motioned for him to come outside. His name was Red Short and the sheriff had known him for years.

59

"Red, you know how this whole town owes Reed Haddok. I know you've heard about the price Beecham put on his head."

Red nodded.

"Well, there's a gang of gunslingers down at the Eagle. My guess is they're on their way to collect that bounty. I want you to get on your horse and ride hard to warn the folks at the ranch that they have company coming."

"I'm on my way and you can count on me," Red said. "We all owe that man and I'll help him any way I can." With that, he mounted his horse and rode hard out of town.

The sheriff then went back to his office and determined to do nothing else about that gang of strangers unless he had to. He was still awake when Mendoza and his men rode out of town at about two o'clock in the morning.

It was Mendoza's plan to hit the ranch about sunup. They rode in one large group. Still feeling the effect of the whiskey and high on the notion of getting rich, they had a feeling of invincibility about them as they rode. They had always taken what they wanted and killed everything and everyone in their path. Haddok and a few ranch hands would be no trouble.

Red had arrived at the Rocking H with the warning about midnight. He decided to stay on through the next day to help out.

Josh immediately called all the men together and they reviewed their plan. They were well armed men with fortified positions and good fields of fire. The bunch on the attack would be in for a surprise.

As Josh dismissed the men to take their positions, he told them, "Shoot to kill. Shoot their horses if you have to and put them afoot. We'll hold our fire til they get in close. When we start to shoot, I want you putting as much lead in the air as you can."

Water was heated to care for the wounded and everything they would need for bandages was laid out. They settled down to wait.

As light gradually spread across the valley, revealing the ranch house and it's buildings, Mendoza and his men sat their horses on the high ground about a mile in front of the ranch. Everything looked quiet and normal. Unknown to them, about ten minutes before they reached the spot where they now were, an outrider had hurried back to the ranch with the warning.

Nothing gave away the reception waiting for the outlaws. Their past had been filled with running roughshod over farmers and people who did not know how to defend themselves. Their success over lesser opponents had lulled them to sleep. They were laughing and talking about what they were going to do with the money when they collected it.

Mendoza made the move and they rode off toward the ranch at a trot. As they neared the out buildings, they pulled their pistols and kicked their horses into a full run. They began to fire at windows and doors as they pulled into the ranch yard.

Josh fired the first shot from behind a wagon beside the ranch house and he emptied the saddle of a rider right in front of him. A blistering fusillade of rifle fire whipped across the yard from ten different firing positions around the ranch. In the initial blast, eight of Mendoza's men died. Filipe Mendoza was one of them. He was hit three times and was dead when he hit the ground. In the following few seconds four more died and five others were wounded. The riders broke off and raced away in a hail of gunfire that continued until they were out of sight. The wounded ones were doing their best to hang onto their saddles as they rode off.

The gunfight didn't last but about two minutes. Two of the ranch hands were wounded, but not seriously. As they walked out into the open after the attack, Josh was quick to give orders.

"Bring a wagon and put their dead on it. Round up their horses and clear the yard. I don't think the others will come back, but we had best be ready. We'll bury their dead later."

The men did as they were told and in a matter of minutes there was no trace of a battle. Josh wanted to take off after the one's who escaped, but his job was to protect the ranch. After he settled down to wait, he reflected on the morning's work. He thought, if they are going to kill Reed Haddok, they had better come up with a better lot than them pilgrims.

Unknown to Josh, Reed had ridden into Prescott about the time the attack broke on the ranch and it was over before he had his first cup of coffee at Fort Misery. Also unknown to Reed, Josh and his men were emptying saddles of men who wanted to kill him.

The quest to kill Haddok had begun.

Reed rode into Prescott about sunup and found the café nearly empty when he walked in. There were only two townfolk at the tables. He asked for coffee and ordered some breakfast. He had left his horse inside Bob Bussler's livery with a feedbag hung around his neck. He needed to talk to the sheriff again and then he planned to ride back to the ranch. He finished his breakfast in quiet and downed two more cups of coffee. He couldn't get Sam off his mind, but he figured that would have to wait til another day.

Reed then paid up and walked out on the street and back toward the livery. He noticed a young man walking toward the café as he walked off. The fact that the feller wore two tied down pistols did not escape him, but he gave the man no indication he had even seen him. When he got to the livery, Bob had arrived and had the doors standing open for business.

"Howdy, friend," Reed said as he walked in. "I stole some of your grain for my horse. I hope you haven't told the sheriff about my stealing."

Bob laughed and came around to give Reed one of those strong handshakes that had come to be his style with him. "You'd have a hard time stealing from me, son. Anything I got is yours and you know it," Bob added as he slapped Reed on the shoulder.

"I appreciate that. You are a friend and I know it."

"It seems you always need all the friends you can get. The sheriff told me he rode out to warn you about the news we got. Where have you been?

I figured you were fighting for your life right now with all them gunslingers who rode out of here during the night headed for your place."

"What are you talking about? I've been over at the Diamond since yesterday and I rode all night coming from there. Who rode out to my ranch?"

"There was a gang of cutthroats, most of them Mexicans, who rode in here yesterday. They were a mean looking lot. They were asking about you. They soaked away the whiskey until late in the night and then rode out."

"I've got to get out there," Reed said, starting for his horse. "There's no telling what kind of shape my men are in."

Bob pulled him up short. "The sheriff sent a rider to warn the ranch shortly after that bunch rode into town."

"Oh well," Reed said as he stopped in his tracks. "If Josh knew they were coming, I'm not worried. I bet they found out what a coon dog feels like after he finally corners the coon." Reed grinned when he thought about that gang riding up to the ranch with Josh expecting them.

"Has there been anybody else looking for me?"

"I've tried to keep my eyes open since I heard about the bounty on you. I've also tried to think back over the last few days. We've had four different situations I planned on getting word to you about. The gang of Mexicans was one of them and the sheriff beat me to the punch on that one. The second one is a stranger who came in here last week to get his horse worked on. The man was a droopy looking sort of a feller with a hawk nose. His horse had a bad hoof and the shoe kept working loose. I fixed his horse for him by using a lightweight shoe. I had to build it up on one side to shift the weight from the weak part of the hoof. That man asked about you. He had already found out where your ranch was from somebody else. The thing that caught my attention was his rifle. I didn't see it good, but it rode about ten to fifteen inches higher in the saddle scabbard than most rifles. He laid his coat across it while he was here and never moved it. It was like he was trying to cover it up. I figure him to be a hired gun and you need to know he could be laid up anywhere waiting on you."

"I needed to know that. You can bet I'll ride the low land until I locate him."

"I helped you a mite. I notched the back right side of the shoe so you would know it if you see it. It looks like this." Bob drew a picture in the dust. "If he's around and leaving tracks, you'll know it."

"That'll help. What about the other two?"

"Well, one of them I feel kind of crazy mentioning. We had a pretty little woman, looked to be about twenty, come in on the stage over a week ago. She's been staying over at the hotel. She hadn't done anything to make me think she was looking for you until this morning right before you got here. She'd just rode off when you walked up. She rented a horse and said she would be gone all day. She knew about the gang that rode out this morning. I warned her not to ride out that way. She said something about the fact that her whole life had been a long trip for nothing. I watched her when she left and she headed toward your place. I don't know how you'd stack up against a mean woman, Reed." Bob smiled , but the warning was in his voice.

"Well, I'll be dog. I'm not sure you can whip a woman and win Bob. I hope you are wrong about her. What's her name?"

"Says it's Stull. Raven Stull!"

"Who else is after me?"

"One sure fire one. A young redheaded gunslinger rode in day before yesterday and he's told it all over town that he's going to kill you."

"Does he wear two guns?" Reed asked.

"Yep! And he's a cocky little feller. He's been struttin all over town and braggin about how fast he is."

65

As Bob was talking they both noticed movement at the big door that opened to the street. Standing square in the middle was the redhead, legs spread and his hands hanging over his sixshooters.

"Would you be Haddok?" he asked. "If you are, I'm calling you. Just walk on out here."

Reed smiled at Bob and said, "I'll be in town for a spell Bob and I would appreciate it if you would shoe my horse for me." He had paid no attention to the man as he walked slowly toward him with his head looking back over his shoulder as he talked to Bob.

The gunslinger had not figured it would happen this way. If this was Haddok, he wasn't acting like it, he thought. Maybe this isn't him at all.

Reed continued his conversation with Bob and kept moving until he was about three paces from the gunslinger. Then he stopped and turned to look at the young man. Reed smiled real big.

"What was it you said?" Reed asked. "I'm sort of hard of hearing and I couldn't make it out back in there."

"I'm Red Cheatham. I'm looking for Haddok. I said, if you was him, I'm calling you out," the gunslinger said loudly.

Red paid little attention that Reed stepped a little closer and leaned toward him like he was trying to hear him better. He did not see the right that came from the hip. It landed square on his jaw and lifted him in the air. He was out cold before he hit the ground.

Reed stepped over him and pulled his knife. He took both hands and sliced the tips of his fingers down to the bone. He was bleeding good and the dirt was already changing colors as it soaked it up. Reed walked over to a sack and wiped the blood off his knife, sat down on a keg, and asked Bob if he would saddle his horse. Bob did and Reed mounted up and looked down at the young man as he spoke to Bob.

"Thanks for everything. When he comes to, tell him to go back where he came from and take up farming or something. Tell him he don't want me to ever see him again."

"I'll do it son. You be careful. Remember, you can always come here if you need to."

Reed nodded and smiled. Then he headed for the Rocking H.

Bob looked down at the young feller who was just beginning to move a little and moan in pain. He thought, you are lucky to have some fingers that will heal up.

Red Cheatham rode out of Prescott that afternoon with both hands wrapped in bandages. The bleeding had about stopped, but they hurt like the devil. It was a long ride to Axel and he couldn't get there soon enough. He was a good way out of town when he pulled up at a high spot on the trail and looked down off a bluff at a thick patch of scrub brush below. He carefully unbuckled his gun belt and without hesitation threw the belt and pistols into the air. His gunfighting days were over, and he had not even had one.

Raven Stull rode toward the Rocking H ranch with a mixture of emotions racing through her mind. She was experiencing a great deal of fear because she was riding alone in a vast land that offered plenty of danger. She had doubts about her mission because she had never done anything to hurt another person. She was on her way to kill a man she did not know. She felt disappointed in the fact that a large number of men were already ahead of her bent on doing the same thing.

She had been in Prescott for just a little over a week and had only accomplished the creation of doubt. She had about decided she shouldn't be there in the first place. She kept away from most people and listened to any conversation that would add to her knowledge about Haddok. It was obvious that he was well thought of in town. The people she overheard around the hotel and in the café spoke of him as a hero. The image of a bad man that needed to be killed had been shattered. She should have known Will Malone would not have told her the truth. She did not know anything about Loyd Beecham until she got to Prescott. His reputation was so bad she felt uncomfortable even though nobody knew why she had come there. Her need for the money that Beecham would pay had kept her in Prescott. Now she was on her way to Haddok's ranch. She wanted to turn around and leave. But if she didn't get the money, she would be right back in a saloon. The twenty thousand dollars was her only hope. She didn't even know if she could kill Haddok. The fact that she was riding toward his place proved she hadn't made up her mind not to try.

She followed the tracks of the men who preceded her. It was easy. But the man at the livery had warned her to steer clear of this part of the country. What would happen to her if she ran up on that gang of gunslingers. It frightened her even more just thinking about it.

She then became more cautious after about two hours on the trail. She figured she had to be getting close to the ranch. She spotted the ranch buildings off in the distance as she rode over the crest of a low hill. The ranch itself set back against the mountains. She sat there scanning the area looking for any indication of trouble. There was evidence of the riders who had come to attack the ranch. Suddenly some movement caught her eye and she got a glimpse of two riders slowly making their way along the trail away from the ranch. They were headed in her direction. They were moving slow and seemed to be checking the trail for something.

She quickly rode back over the hill away from the ranch and dismounted. She looked around and found the right spot. Sitting down on the ground, she pulled one leg around until it was pointed in an unnatural direction. She then took a handful of dirt and rubbed it into her hairline and on her forehead, lay back with her head away from the approaching riders, closed her eyes, and waited. It seemed like an eternity before they came up.

"What the heck is that?" one of the men asked.

She heard the horses rushing toward her and felt the hands of the men as they straightened her body and gently lifted her head.

"She's out cold," one voice said.

"She don't appear to be shot," the other added.

"Her horse must have throwed her. Get me your canteen."

Raven felt a wet cloth gently rub her face. She remained motionless.

"I'll stay here with her. You better go get a buckboard so we can get her to the ranch."

"I'll be back with some help. You keep your eyes peeled. Some of that pack might still be around."

Raven heard the rider leave. She knew she didn't want to do any talking until she got to the ranch. It was not long until she heard the sounds of a wagon and other riders.

"I believe she's hurt bad," the man holding her said. "What should we do, boss?"

When Raven heard the word boss, she thought, is Haddok here?

A new voice spoke, "Be careful with her and get her onto the wagon. We'll get her to the ranch and then send for the doctor."

Strong hands lifted her gently and placed her on the wagon. Someone was still holding her head.

"Get her horse and come on," the new voice said.

The wagon moved out at a slow pace, but even with that the ride was rough. Raven began to feign a few low moans and move her hands slightly.

The man holding her head shouted, "She's starting to come around a little."

When the wagon came to a stop, Raven opened her eyes and looked around as if she was frightened. A tall man stood looking down at her and smiled. When he spoke, she knew the voice to be that of the last man to arrive. He sounded so calm when he spoke.

"Don't be afraid. You must have fallen from your horse. You're at the Rocking H ranch. My name is Josh Spencer. You just relax. We're going to take you into the house and make you comfortable."

Raven looked at him with a dazed glare and did not respond. She closed her eyes as they carried her into the house. So, the voice had belonged to Josh Spencer. She knew him to be Haddok's partner from the talk she heard back in town. Where is Haddok, she thought? Surely he's not dead.

They took her into a room and placed her on a bed. A Mexican woman came in with a bowl of water and wet a cloth. She placed the cloth on Raven's forehead. Raven didn't want to recover too quickly. She mumbled a few words and continued to fake the grogginess.

Josh Spencer soon came into the room and sat on the edge of the bed. He touched Raven and she opened her eyes.

"Maria will take care of you. Just relax. You are safe here."

Raven whispered, "Thank you."

A ranch hand interrupted them to tell Josh that Haddok was riding in. Josh stood up and left the room, turning to Maria as he closed the door, "Stay with her."

Raven slowly moved her hand to her side and casually felt the bottle in the pocket of her skirt. Will I get a chance to use it? she thought.

Reed rode up to the ranch from a different direction than usual. He had taken Bob Bussler's words to heart. He held to the low ground and traveled where there was no existing trail. Reed had taken the time while riding to think through all that was taking place. He hoped none of his men had been hurt.

When Reed rode into the ranch yard the men rushed out to gather around him.

"You should have been here, boss," one of them said. "You missed the party."

"Yep! You sure did," another said. "It was like an old fashioned hoe-down around here for a little while."

A man Reed didn't recognize walked over to shake his hand. "I'm Red Short," he said. "The sheriff sent me out to warn you folks. I decided to stay and help. I work for Dean Rawls over at the Double O. He don't know where I am, but he won't mind. He says almost every day that he owes you."

"Thanks for helping, Red," Reed said. "You tell your boss that I'll hire you if he's mad." Reed laughed as he said it and all the men laughed too.

Josh had walked up to listen to the conversation. "Reed, we've got twelve dead men from that gang laid out over in the barn. It looked like three or four more were hit and hanging on when they rode off. There was over twenty of them in all."

"Did we get anybody hurt?"

"A couple of the guys got nicked a bit. Nothing serious. They both could fight right now," Josh answered.

"Which way did they ride off?" Reed asked.

"They rode out that way," Josh answered as he pointed to the northeast. "I didn't chase them because I didn't know exactly how many they had. I didn't want to leave the ranch unprotected. I figured we could go after them after things settled down and we knew what we were dealing with."

Reed turned to the men, "I really appreciate what you've done here today. You put your life on the line and I'll always be grateful for you. I won't forget it. Now ya'll get back to your positions and keep an eye out for anything. I need to talk with Josh privately."

They all moved away to their defensive positions and Reed walked with Josh over to the porch where they both sat down.

"I'm going after them. I should be able to catch up pretty soon if they are dragging their wounded."

"I'm going with you," Josh responded.

"No, Josh. I need you to stay here and take care of the ranch."

"Now wait a minute. I'm not lettin you go off alone."

"I'll be all right and you know it. You just don't want to miss the fun. If we knew what to expect, it would be different. For all we know, there might be another gang of outlaws on their way here right now. Twenty thousand dollars will bring out a lot of snakes."

"Well, we'll be ready if they do."

"While I was in town, Bob Bussler filled me in on a few things I need to warn you about. There's a lone rider Bob figures to be an ambusher. He has a long barreled rifle, probably a fifty caliber, and has been asking about the ranch. Bob put a shoe on his horse and he did us a favor. He notched the

73

right rear part of the shoe. It looks like this." Reed drew him the pattern in the dirt off the edge of the porch. "Have the men to keep an eye out for any tracks like that. I'd also like you to have them check the hill behind the ranch real good. That's how I got to Beecham and it would be the perfect place for this man to lay up and shoot."

Josh asked, "Do you know anymore about him?"

"Bussler said he was a frail man with a hawk nose. That's all I know."

"We'll keep an eye out for his sign."

"There's another thing. He said there was a young woman who came into town and he was a little concerned she might be looking to claim the money too."

"Well, what about that. We've got one in the house right now. The boys found her back up the trail a little while before you rode in. It appeared her horse had thrown her. She was out cold. We brought her here. Maria is looking after her."

"Check her out. She might have a funeral in mind for me." Reed gave him that grin he had come to expect.

Josh grinned back. "She's a pretty little thing. She ain't carrying no gun that I can tell. Maybe she planned on huggin' you to death."

Reed laughed. "Just the same, you check her out."

"Already planned to," he winked. "Seen plenty of folks get bucked off a horse and more than a few get knocked out. Never seen a one get throwed into the kind of rocks she was layin in without a cut, bump, or scratch. I figured on giving her a little time and then I'll pin her down."

After Reed left, Josh called the men together and filled them in about the ambusher. He didn't say anything about the woman. He figured to handle that himself.

He then went back inside the house and poured himself a cup of coffee. This had been a busy day and it still was early. To this point, it had all gone well. He had real doubts about allowing Reed to go after the remnants of the gang alone. He could be going up against six or seven gunmen. He knew Reed better than anyone and he had no doubt about his ability. It was just hard to let him go alone.

His mind turned to the woman. He thought, surely such a pretty thing couldn't be a killer. Maybe she has a reason for being here.

Maria soon came out. "The senorita is feeling better. She will be up in a moment."

"Thanks Maria. What do you think about her? I mean, do you think she was really hurt?"

"I'm not sure senor. I think maybe she is being a woman. She may be working her magic," Maria said with a laugh.

Josh laughed and thought, Maria has noticed it too. He drank his coffee and waited.

Raven soon opened the door and stepped into the room. She was more beautiful than Josh had thought. She had a look of fear on her face as she crossed the room and took a chair across from him. She kept her eyes down as her shaking hands placed a small bottle on the table in front of her.

75

"Mister Spencer, I need to talk to you," she said.

"You can sure do that. But you've got to stop that mister stuff. Just call me Josh."

She smile slightly and looked him in the eyes. Her voice was broken as she spoke. "Josh, I've done something horrible." She began to sob.

Josh stood up and walked around to sit beside her. He put his strong hand on her shoulder. "Now, calm down. You are safe here and among friends. You can tell me anything you want to."

She wiped her eyes. "I need to tell you why I came. To do that, I must tell you about my life." She began to talk and Josh listened with interest for over an hour. She ended with her years of waiting on tables in the saloon.

"Josh, I hated every minute of it. You can believe me or not, but not one time did I ever allow one of these men to use me. I could see what it had done to the other women. There have been a few times when I felt so low I wished I was dead. I know you think all this is crazy and you are wondering what it has to do with my being here."

"I'm glad you are telling me. You need to talk and I'm better at listening than talking. So, you go on."

"Thank you. My life was about as low as it could get when the talk in the saloon turned to a twenty thousand dollar price a man in Santa Fe had put on Reed Haddok's life. I was told he was a bad man that needed to be killed. I've never hurt anybody in my life. All of a sudden the money seemed like my ticket out. You see this bottle, Josh? It contains poison. It's the bottle my mother gave to me to use if the Indians got to me. It's all I got that mother ever gave me. I've kept it through the years. There have been times when the easiest thing I could have done would be to drink it. Each time I thought about it, I would also think that life for me would get better. So, I'd save my bottle and figure if it got too bad, I could always drink it. When I thought about the money Loyd Beecham would pay for someone to kill

76

Haddok, I made up my mind I could do it to get out of that saloon. I took the money I had saved and bought a stage ticket to Prescott. What I'm telling you is that I came here to kill your friend."

Josh had been listening without any sign of emotion, but down inside himself, he was taking it all in. He wasn't good at much. Judging character and honesty was one thing he could do better than most. That was why he had stepped in to help Reed Haddok's father a long time ago and really the reason he was here in Arizona. He said to her, "Go on. I'm listening."

"When I got to Prescott I began to learn that Reed Haddok was not a bad person at all. Everybody around here seems to love him. I also learned that Loyd Beecham was the bad man. I'm so ashamed of myself. I should have left as soon as I learned this. But where would I go? The money was so important to me I came here anyway." She began to cry.

"Go ahead. Tell me the whole story," Josh said calmly.

"Josh, I didn't fall from my horse. I staged that so you would bring me here. I thought I could get close enough to put this in something Reed Haddok was drinking." She pushed the bottle toward Josh.

"Please destroy this. I was wrong and no reason was good enough to kill someone. I know that you must hate me. If you will allow me, I want to go back to town and catch the first stage I can out of here. I would understand it if you turned me over to the sheriff."

"I'm sorry, but I can't let you go," Josh said.

"I thought I was asking a lot of you."

"Oh, you don't understand. I'm not keeping you here to punish you. It's dangerous out there right now and I'm not about to let you ride off alone. I need my men here and I can't leave. You are safe here and you will be free to leave whenever you like after this mess settles down. If it will make you feel better, I believe you. I can tell you Reed will too."

**She smiled for the first time and it would have melted an anvil. It sure melted Josh's heart.**

**R**eed rode north for about two miles and then circled to the east. He was careful to stay off the high ground. He hit the trail of the retreating gunmen about where he'd figured to find it and it was easy to follow.

He rode at a steady clip. He figured they had four hours on him and they would probably ride until late and hole up somewhere. The direction they were headed told him about where they would be come sundown. Reed found two places where a rider had broken off on high ground and watched their back trail for a spell. They were being careful and that meant that he would have to go slow the closer he got to them.

Riding gave Reed time to think. The side of him that came to the top when he got pushed had been having a fit since he left Prescott. Reed thought, they may have figured to collect that twenty thousand dollars pretty easy. Up to now they have had it easy. When I catch up to them, I'm going to teach them that killing a man is a hard way to make a living.

It was getting late in the afternoon when Reed got close enough to the mountains to make out the distinctions of the landscape. He pulled up in some trees and got his eyeglass out of the saddle bags. He had been riding off to the side of their trail for a while and knew the obvious cut through the mountains they would probably take. It followed a stream that long ago had provided a natural trail through the gigantic peaks.

Reed glassed the area and found the cut. He could make out the mist from the fast flowing stream. He studied the area carefully and finally spotted what he was looking for. Back up the cut a ways there was a faint trail of smoke rising up out of the trees. They had built a fire. Reed stepped down from the saddle and rustled some jerked beef from his saddle bags and sat down to wait for dark. A plan was developing in his mind. There was a part of him that kept saying, forget the plan and just ride in shooting and get it over with. He fought that urge.

Reed continued to study the area with his glass in the fleeting light. He knew they would have somebody watching their trail. Reed wanted to know where he would be. He had picked a couple of likely places.

Sure enough. A little after dark he saw a match flare up. He also caught the sporadic glow of a cigarette. The guard was a smoker. That always helped. He was in an outcropping of rocks that stood about twenty feet above the trail. The guard had a good view of the trail from there and could warn his friends of any approaching riders.

He was about a quarter of a mile from Reed's position and would be his first target. Reed planned to get him quietly and then move in on the rest.

Reed was in no hurry. He wanted his enemies to have enough time for their weariness to set in. A night of drinking and a morning of getting shot up, with a day of riding thrown in, was bound to have left them a little used.

Around midnight Reed began to make his move. He led his horse down off the ridge and stayed to the low ground as he moved toward their camp. It was a fairly dark night and Reed wasn't worried. He tied his horse about three hundred paces from the place where he had spotted the guard.

Haddok removed his boots and left them with his hat by his horse. He quietly worked around and up to the level he had spotted the guard, stopping often to listen. Reed smelled the man's cigarette before he saw its glow. The silhouette of the man showed he was seated on a rock facing in the opposite direction. He finished his smoke and threw the butt down. Reed saw the sprinkle of sparks as it bounced off a rock. He stood motionless about twenty paces from him and waited.

After a few minutes, what Reed had been waiting for happened: a rustle as the man began to roll another cigarette. Reed softly moved forward, feeling the ground with his sock feet before putting down weight. He eased his knife from his belt and held it low to his side. The last few steps were quick. Reed was walking on rock now.

The match flared up to light the cigarette, but it never reached the man's mouth. Reed's left hand crushed the freshly rolled cigarette into his mouth as he covered it to stifle any scream. The same instant that Reed's hand covered his mouth, his other hand thrust the knife into his neck. Then he pushed it away from him, effectively ripping the man's throat open. He held him tightly until there was no life left. The only sound was a low gurgle.

Reed lowered the body to the rocks, wiped his hands and knife on his clothes, and quietly retreated to his horse. Donning boots and hat, he listened for a few minutes, but heard no sound. After checking the loads in his pistol and rifle, he led his horse out toward where he was certain their camp would be.

Reed could make out the low glow of their fire. It was almost too quiet. He tied his horse to some brush, took his rifle, and headed toward the fire. One man was seated there with his left side toward Haddok. There were about six people in bedrolls.

Without hesitation Reed lifted his rifle and shot the man seated by the fire. He never knew what hit him. He then immediately shifted the aim to the bedrolls. Shell after shell riddled the men who were fighting to get out and into action. They gave up the right to be treated with respect when they attacked my ranch, Reed thought. I would have taken them on one at a time. They chose the method and they could die by the method. It didn't bother him one bit.

It was over nearly before it started. Reed could hear some moans, but there was no movement. He walked carefully with his rifle at the ready. As he got closer, he decided to uncover them and make sure they were dead. Reed walked close to the fire and was about to lean over to pull the blanket off one of the men when there was a boom and flash of light from his left. The force of the bullet knocked Haddok sideways and to the ground. It was a wicked blow and he knew he was hit hard. He managed to fire three shots in the direction the shot came from. Reed crawled back the way he had come.

He got to his horse and managed to pull himself into the saddle. He was trying his best to hang on. But before he could tie himself to the saddle, everything went black. Reed fell from the horse, losing consciousness somewhere between the saddle and the ground.

The hands were strong that lifted the wounded man to his horse and draped him over the saddle. A cold wet cloth had been pushed into the wound to stop the bleeding. Miles stood between him and any hope of staying alive. The same strong hands led the horse away from the pool of blood and up the mountain.

**H**addok had been gone about six hours and it was getting on into the afternoon when Samantha rode into the ranch yard at the Rocking H. Some of the men came out to meet her.

She swung down from the saddle and handed the reins to one. "Please put him up for me," she said. "Where's Reed?"

"He's gone after what's left of a bunch of gunslingers that hit the ranch early this morning," a cowhand responded.

Josh and Raven came out of the house and Samantha ran to Josh and hugged him.

"Man, it's good to see you Sam," Josh said as he returned the hug. "I thought Reed wanted you to stay away until this thing settles down."

"Oh Josh, I've been a woman fool. I blamed Reed for all this trouble and let him ride off thinking I wasn't behind him. I had to come. I plan on staying here until it's over and I want him to know that anybody who tries to kill him will have to be good enough to kill both of us. Why, it was Reed's loyalty to my father that got him in all this mess."

Josh squeezed her again and grinned, "I've known you had grit from the first time I met you Sam. And believe me, Reed knows that too. You haven't failed him."

"Oh yes I have. You don't understand. I acted like a spoiled kid. He was thinking about our safety and I was thinking about myself. I've got to talk to him."

"That's going to be hard to do right now. We got hit by about twenty riders this morning. We had been warned they were on their way and we were ready. We killed twelve and wounded three or four more. When Reed got here, he asked me to stay and protect the ranch. He rode after them."

Sam suddenly noticed Raven. "Who is this?"

"Raven Stull, meet Samantha Forbes," Josh said.

Raven walked over and extended her hand. It was more of a comforting hand than a handshake.

She looked at Josh with a look that clearly said, who is this woman and what is she doing here?

Josh smiled. "Come on inside. Raven's story is a long one and we might as well get out of the sun while we tell it."

Inside, around the table, Josh related the course of events that had brought Raven there. Sam was quiet for a few minutes and then looked at the young woman across the table. "Raven, I can't say I understand what you've been through. I've never had to be on my own. I can tell you that I understand how you made the mistake that brought you here. I'm anxious for you to meet Reed Haddok. You would never have a better friend than him. As far as your plan to kill him, that's water down the creek as far as I'm concerned. I won't hold it against you."

"Thank you," Raven said quietly.

"Now, let's figure out what we are going to do about this man I love," Sam said.

"For now, all we do is wait," Josh said. "He told me to stay here and give him until dark tomorrow before I send anybody out to look for him."

"I know he can take care of himself," Sam added. "I guess we might as well get some food on the table and keep the coffee hot."

The women busied themselves with supper and Josh made his rounds checking on the defensive positions. He talked to each man and encouraged them to be alert. They would come to eat in shifts.

After supper, Josh, Sam and Raven talked late into the night before turning in. When Sam and Raven got up the next morning, Josh was already gone. He would spend the day riding and looking for the notched-shoe track that Reed had told him about. The sun was setting when Josh returned.

"I just know something has happened to him," Sam said as Josh came in.

"It's a little early to get all worked up, Sam. If he don't ride in tonight, I'll take some of the men and trail him," Josh replied.

"But what if he's out there somewhere hurt. If it was me out there, or you, I know he would be looking for us."

"I've thought about that. It nearly killed me to let him go off by himself. I know which way they were headed and there ain't but one easy way through the mountains in that direction. If he don't show up by midnight, then I'll ride out. I can cut their trail at sunup and be there soon after. I figured that bunch would hole up somewhere with their wounded men. If they did, then Reed caught up to them late yesterday. Knowing him, he went to work on them last night. I know I can't ease your mind. You just remember that he will take a mite more killing than most folks."

"Oh, I know he's tough. This is just so hard on me, especially after I let him leave the way I did."

"You just don't go diggin no grave for him. It'l take a whole lot of dirt to cover him up."

Raven listened and wished she had someone to love and someone to worry about her. She realized that she was becoming emotionally involved with these people and their trouble. She had absolutely no right to do so.

Midnight came and no Reed. Josh lined up three men to ride with him. They were stepping into their saddles when Sam and Raven came out.

"Find him, Josh. Tell him I'm here waiting," Sam said.

Josh nodded and as he turned to ride out, his eyes fell on Raven and she mouthed, "Be careful." He thought as he rode out, first time that's ever happened. I believe I might.

They rode at a good pace through the rest of the night and the sun had been up about an hour as they were nearing the mountains. They had located the trail shortly after first light. They topped a rise and spotted circling buzzards in the sky.

"We've got something up there," one of the riders said.

"Let's hope it ain't Reed," Josh said.

They slowed their pace and rode carefully. As they came up close to the stream, Josh pulled up and dismounted. The other men followed his lead. They ground hitched their horses and moved forward, pistols ready for action.

"This place looks a mess," Josh said as he looked over the deathly scene. "Look for Reed, but be careful with the sign. If he ain't here, we are going to have to sort this all out and see what happened."

They went through the camp and counted the bodies. There were eight dead men around the campfire. It was hard to tell which ones had the old wounds, but it didn't matter. They were all dead. They saw no sign of Reed. They spread out and began to circle the camp looking for anything that would fill in the story.

They found another dead man about fifty paces from the fire. They stood looking at him in amazement. He was lying on his back, an arrow in his chest. That didn't make sense to them. They continued to circle and finally found the place where Reed had started shooting. The ground was littered with empty shells.

"Look here, Josh," one of them said.

The grass was stained with blood.

"He was hit," Josh whispered. "It looks bad. He crawled this way.

86

Yes, look at this. He crawled through here."

They followed the blood trail.

"His horse was tied here. Looks like he managed to get on and head off that way," Josh said.

They walked carefully, checking the ground and suddenly stopped with a sad awareness.

"He fell off," a cowhand said.

"There's a lot more blood here. But something is different. The grass is all mashed down around him. Somebody was helping him," Josh spit out. "Look this way. Somebody put him on his horse and led it out through these rocks." He pointed up the side of the mountain. "Ya'll gather up these men's horses and gear and we'll take them back. There's a high wash bank over there." He pointed toward the stream bed. "Lay their bodies under the bank and cave it in over them. You can put some rocks on top to keep the vultures away. I'm going to follow the trail of Reed's horse if I can. I'll come back to get you when I see where it leads."

The men got busy and Josh started out. He was walking the trail out. It was easier that way because there wasn't much to see. He went up and over the mountain and was making pretty good time until he came upon a small feeder creek to a larger stream below. The horse had entered the water and the creek bottom was solid stone. There was no more sign. He squatted and looked the area over. He figured they had gone upstream.

As he scanned the area, he noticed something in the mud on the far bank across from him. He walked out in the water that was almost waist deep and waded across. When he got close, he looked down and saw a footprint. It was a mocassin clad footprint. Josh grinned and thought, he left that for me. The owner of that arrow down there in that man's chest has my friend and he wanted me, or somebody, to know. The only footprint he left and he did that on purpose.

87

Josh then got back across the creek and sat down. I could probably look the rest of the day and not find any more sign, he thought. He led me to this spot and told me to back off.

Josh headed back down to the camp and found the men finishing up. "We found another one back up there," one of the men said. "He must have been the lookout. Reed cut his throat."

Josh told them what he had found. "He was still alive or the Indian would never have taken him. We won't find them. That Indian is good. It was like he was leading me to the spot where he left his sign. I think we'd be better off going back to the ranch and waiting this out. Reed Haddok is as tough as a lighter knot. If that Indian can get him to some place where he can care for him, his chances are good. These Indians have cared for their battle wounds forever and their medicine is pretty good."

Reed's mind was spinning in and out of reality. Each time his thinking became real, his pain did too. He had vague recollections of being lifted and placed across a saddle. The hands that touched him had been strong. The voice that spoke to him had been in a language he did not know. Then the darkness that came over him after that had been welcomed.

Reed remembered a feeling as if someone had pushed a red hot rod through his side. The pain was so unbearable that he rushed back into the darkness of his unconsciousness.

Now his awareness flickered back, but things were different. Everything was still and quiet. It was dark and there was a small light somewhere. His eyes would not focus and he had a bitter taste in his mouth. He felt numb, as if no part of his body would follow the command of his mind. Reed fought the urge to panic and forced his eyes to look toward the light. Briefly, just before his eyelids closed and he drifted off again, he saw a shadowy figure kneeling by a small fire.

In time, that he had no way of measuring, he opened his eyes again. He spoke, but there was no answer. He then moved his hands and was relieved that they worked. Reed felt of his body and found himself naked. He had been placed on a blanket of animal skins and was covered with another. His hands then went to his left side where the pain was the worst. It was wrapped in a poulace of some sort. Reed barely remembered being shot and pulling himself onto his horse.

A small fire was burning nearby and Reed could hear water dripping into a pool in the distance. He was in a cave.

At his side were two pottery bowls and he dipped his finger in one and tasted it. It held water. He lifted the bowl and drank. The second one held a bitter tasting brew. Trusting whoever rescued him, Reed lifted that bowl and forced himself to drink. It was powerful. In a matter of minutes he drifted off to sleep.

The next time Reed regained consciousness there was a third bowl sitting near the fire. He brought the bowl to his lips and savored the soupy broth as it permeated his body.

The dressing on his side had been changed and the pain had diminished. Reed knew better than to move around too much. His mind was still fuzzy but he drank some more water, followed by the concoction that produced the deep sleep. As he drifted off, he felt warm and safe.

Reed repeated this sequence of events more times than he could calculate. He had lost all track of time and had no idea how long he had been in the cave.

He did know when the crises had passed, however, when he awoke to a real need to relieve himself. Being careful, he managed to crawl a few feet away from the fire, then slowly returned to his bed of skin blankets. After resting a few moments, he noticed a slab of roasted meat by the fire and he grabbed it like a wild animal. It was cooked rare and the grease, blood and flesh was an infusion of strength into his body. Then he slept again, this time without the herbal potion.

The next time he woke, his clothes lay beside him, clean and dried stiff by the sun. More meat and some fried bread was by the fire. After eating, he began the process of getting the use of his limbs back. Reed carefully moved his legs and arms in intervals. After about an hour of this and a drink of water, he slept again.

90

Each time he woke he was stronger than before. When he opened his eyes this time he slowly removed the bandage that covered his wound to find a puckering hole that was almost healed over. He carefully replaced the bandage and decided it was time to get some clothes on. He managed the pants and socks before fatigue set in. Covering himself in the blankets, he fell asleep.

Unknown to Reed, three weeks had passed since he had been brought to the cave. To him it seemed about ten days. When he was finally able to stand and walk a little, he ventured to the mouth of the cave and gazed out over a beautiful stand of large trees covering the side of a mountain. He later discovered his horse further back in the large cavern and was surprised that it had good water and had been brought plenty of grass to feed on. Reed's pistol and knife were draped over his saddle lying back against the wall.

From that day, food was left at the mouth of the cave. That is, except for one night. Reed had crouched down at the entrance intent on meeting whoever was helping him. But this time, the food was left hanging from a tree rather than the entrance. Reed laughed to himself when he woke up the next morning and found it. He's pretty good, he thought to himself. I don't guess I'll see him til he wants me to.

Reed grew stronger each day and found his daily food supply a greater distance from the cave every morning. Reed was now wearing his pistol and had spent some time working on getting it into action.

Reed thought a lot about the person who had nursed him through this horrible time. He desperately wanted to thank him, but was becoming convinced it would never happen.

Reed then began scouting the area. Returning from one of these outings, he was shocked to find his horse and saddle gone. Rushing back outside he saw his horse disappear into the brush.

Reed laughed to himself and thought, he's telling me it's time to go. He then reached into his belt for his most prized possession. His grandpaw had made the knife back in Tennessee and it had been his constant companion since he had been old enough to handle it. Reed ran his fingers along the ten inch blade, then knelt and placed it on top of the skin blankets. It was the only way Reed knew to say thanks.

Turning quickly for fear that he would change his mind about the knife, he hurried out of the cave and down toward where he had seen his horse disappear. Reed found the tracks easily and followed them toward the sound of a stream. It was about forty feet wide, running deep and swift. In the distance Reed heard the sound of a waterfall which drowned out all other sounds as he approached. By this time Reed figured he was at least three miles from the cave.

Mist from the fall was rising a good thirty feet above the level of the stream and a beautiful rainbow was glistening in the sunlight. Reed paused, wondering which way to go. He suddenly spotted the tracks of his horse and scrambled down a bank and followed them until they turned abruptly and led straight to the entrance of a narrow cave about three feet wide and eight feet tall. It led directly beneath the falls. A ledge about four feet wide led to the left and Reed took it, pushing through the falling water. It was so cold that it shocked him for a moment and when he focused his eyes, he spotted his horse tied to a sapling.

Reed stepped into the saddle, looked around, and nudged his horse. He felt he was leaving a friend he did not even know.

"Come on boy, let's go home."

Josh Spencer had been out looking for his friend every day for three weeks. He would take a section of the land and scour it for sign. On this day, he was in the mountains to the north of where Reed had disappeared. He was moving back and forth searching the ground. He had two motives. He wanted to find Reed and he also wanted to find any sign of the ambusher Reed had told him about. He had failed in finding his friend, but he had not failed in finding the horse tracks with the notched shoe. The man was still on the ranch. He was also good. There were no other signs that Josh could trail.

Another hour passed and Josh was about to give up for the day. He set his horse back in the shadows and looked the valley over that spread before him. Suddenly, out of nowhere, a rider appeared. He chuckled to himself and pulled around to move his horse out of sight into the thick brush. He decided to have a little fun.

Josh watched Reed work his way across the valley. He had in mind to let Reed ride past him and then spook him a little. This would sound like kid stuff to some folks, but it was a part of the life they shared and both had done it to each other many times before. Josh could hardly wait.

As Reed came closer, he suddenly stopped and sat in the saddle for a couple of minutes resting.

"You're getting old Josh."

"How'd you know I was here?" Josh asked as he came out of the brush, a smile on his face.

"Why, I've been listening to you breathing for half a mile," Reed said laughing.

They both piled out of their saddles and met in a hug that almost shook the mountain. Stepping back, his hands still clasping Josh's shoulders, Reed said, "Man, you look mighty good to me." He noticed the moisture in his friend's eyes and looked away for a moment. That's something he and Josh had never shared.

"You look a little gaunt, but still a sight for sore eyes. Everybody figured you dead except me and Sam. I knew you was too tough to die and Sam said there was no way you was going to get by with not marrying her," Josh said, with a grin taking the place of emotion.

"Is she all right?"

"Yep! She's been at the ranch since the day after you rode off after them killers. She says she ain't never leaving."

"I've lost track of time. How long has it been?"

"It's been twenty-eight days. That's a long time. Let's find us a spot in the shade and do some talking."

They walked their horses back into the trees and found an open spot and sat down..

"I found them gunslingers the day I rode out," Reed said. "I waited for dark before I moved in. It was a easy job because them that hadn't been wounded were tuckered out. I killed their lookout and moved in with them rolled up asleep. They were a little more cautious than I figured. The one that got me was probably a lookout. I hadn't counted on that. I got off a couple of shots at him when I went down, but I figure he got away."

"Nope! We found him with an arrow buried in his chest."

"Well, I'll be dog. My friend must have finished my job."

"The feller that took you off was an Indian. I trailed ya'll for a spell

94

and just before the trail petered out, he left me a clear sign, one footprint in the mud."

Reed laughed. "He don't do nothing without it being on purpose. I don't hardly remember anything after I got hit." He pulled out his shirt and showed Josh his wound. "I came to in a cave and the Indian has been nursing me back to life. I've never even seen him or talked to him the whole time. He gave me their medicine and brought me food. For some reason he took me in and kept me alive. I owe him my life."

"When I knew that an Indian had you, my hope went up. They have ways that we would be smart to learn about."

"There's a lot more about this I'll tell you later. What's going on at the ranch?"

"Well first, I got a letter from my old friend Doc. You remember him?"

Reed nodded.

"He must have come to Prescott after you run Beecham off. He learned I was with you and he sent me his letter from Texas. He said that the Malone feller handling the offer on your head back in Santa Fe had been killed by an unknown gunman. He also said Beecham was using the name Frank Lain in Santa Fe and that he left Santa Fe and was headed somewhere near Fort Defiance in Arizona. The word is that only three people had signed on to kill you. The feller whose gang hit the ranch was Filipe Mendoza. We were lucky on that one. The ambusher is another one. He goes by the name Executioner. I have heard about him more than once and he has the reputation of being good. He's a pure killer of the worst sort. The last is a woman by the name of Raven Stull. The good news is that we've taken care of two of them already."

"What do you mean?"

"Mendoza's gang is gone and I'm gonna marry the woman," Josh said with a grin.

"What?"

"Oh, she don't know it yet." Josh then told Reed the story. "She's a fine lady, Bud. I aim to see that she has some better days in her life."

"Can't say as I blame you. I knew you'd get tired of hanging out with me some day."

"That ain't happened yet and I don't plan on leaving you by yourself. Why, without me, you'd still have a gang of gunslingers and a mean woman after your hide." Josh laughed and it felt good to enjoy the company of his friend.

"What about the ambusher? Still around?"

"Yep! He's around and he's good. We find his sign every now and then. It's always off the road to town and west of the ranch. There's no doubt he's waiting for you to show up."

"Well, you've taken care of two. I guess it's my turn. Let's go home. By the way, was Doc the gunman that took care of Malone?"

"He didn't say, but I figure he was."

"I'm gonna have to meet that gent some day. I owe him a debt."

96

It had been a long day for Samantha. Like all the others, she had spent it trying to stay busy and keep hope alive. She and Raven had now become good friends. They had spent the day doing chores around the house and after supper they sat on the porch until well after dark. They soon decided to call it a night.

"Sam! Come in here," they heard Josh yell as they were getting ready for bed.

As Sam rushed into the living room, her smiling man was standing there with outstretched arms. She ran across the room, crying like a little girl.

Raven soon followed and gave Josh a hug.

"I'm so proud you found him Josh," she said.

"As usual, he found me," Josh replied, laughing. Hugging was kind of new for Josh and he was liking it. There had never been a woman in his life and he didn't rightly know how to handle it. "You sure do look beautiful," Reed said as he looked into Samantha's eyes. "I'd a come sooner if I'd known you were here."

They stood for a long time saying nothing. Josh broke the silence.

"Raven. we might as well turn in. I've got a feeling these two have a lot to say to each other."

They then went to their rooms, leaving the couple alone.

"Reed, I was afraid I would never get to tell you this," Sam said as they sat down at the table. " I must tell you before we talk about anything else."

Reed looked a little puzzled.

"I was wrong to let you leave the way I did when you came to warn us. I know the reason you are facing all this trouble is because you helped my father when he needed a friend."

"Now, listen Sam," Reed interrupted.

"You listen. It will never happen again. I love you. I'm going to stand by you no matter what. If somebody wants to kill you, they'll just have to kill me too."

"I'm strong enough to handle this trouble and I just want you to be here when it's finished," Reed said, gripping her hand.

"I'll be here."

"Sam, you know I love you. When we get this thing settled, I'll take you home and ask your father for your hand."

"He says I haven't been worth much since you showed up at the Diamond." She laughed and her eyes filled with tears. "Now, tell me where you've been?"

Reed then told her how he was rescued.

"You mean you never saw or talked with the Indian?" Sam asked.

"No, I didn't. But I'll never rest until I do. I'll have to be careful, though. I've got a feeling he took a big risk taking care of me. A lot of it is a puzzle, but I'll find a way to thank him. Meanwhile, I've got a man on my ranch who wants to shoot me in the back. Taking care of him is my first job."

"Reed, I want you to rest up a few days before you start out."

"I'm getting stronger each day. I can't wait too long. I'm going to spend tomorrow here in the house and get as much of Maria's good cooking

98

down me as I can. Then I'll head out that night and introduce this pilgrim to the world of being hunted. If he's on the ranch, I'll find him."

Reed slept late and woke up to the smell of food. After breakfast he laid out his plans to Josh. "I'll leave out about midnight. I want to be on the high ground west of the ranch come daylight so I can see if I can spot him. I'm going to stay out there til I find him. Ya'll will need to fill my saddle bags with plenty of jerked beef and I'll need an extra canteen of water. Put a bag of grain in for my horse. I also need a knife. I left mine for the Indian. It was all I had to leave him."

"I know what that knife meant to you, Bud," Josh said. "It must have been hard to do."

"I know that knife will be used by a man that would make me proud."

"You can use mine for now. You get a lot more good out of a knife than I do anyway."

The day passed quickly and Reed slept most of the afternoon. After another big meal, they talked well into the night. Finally Reed said, "It's time to go. Ya'll keep the table set for me."

**R**euben Partlow had a good view of the ranch as Mendoza and his men attacked. As he watched the deathly scene unfold, two emotions flooded his mind.

One was that of great relief. He did not want to have come all this way just to watch someone else kill Haddok and claim the bounty on his head. The other was of great respect that came close to fear. The ranch was well prepared for this attack and that meant he would have to be very cautious or he too could end up dead.

All he knew about Haddok was that he rode a big dark horse with four white stocking feet. He had not seen such a horse and figured that his quarry was safe. For now, Partlow felt it best to get away from the ranch. Retreating, he kept to the low land and made his way back to his campsite.

He felt he had made a good choice, a closed hollow that could be entered from a rocky stream bed. The stream was a couple of feet in its deepest parts and this made it impossible for anyone to trail him. He followed the stream for a good half mile before he left it and when he did, it was back against the grain of the stream and through some thick brush that lined the bank.

The trees and deadfall were so thick around him that nobody could get through without making a racket. He was in an ideal place to get back and forth from a good firing position in about an hour's time. All he needed now was time and Haddok in his rifle sights.

Partlow sat down by his fire and contemplated the situation. He had witnessed a well-defended ranch make easy work of what looked like about twenty riders. This would not be an easy job. His initial reaction had been to wait a couple of days and then ride out. But the money on Haddok's head clouded his mind and he settled on staying in camp a few days to let the dust settle. After things settled back down on the ranch, his chances would be much better.

He stayed in camp for a week and then rode into Prescott for supplies. He arrived about mid-morning and after buying his provisions he made his way to Fort Misery for lunch. He sat alone and mostly ate and listened. The talk was still stirring about the attack on the Rocking H.

"Haddok went off after what was left of the attackers and he has completely disappeared," he heard one gent say.

Another added, "They found all the men dead that Haddok trailed. Haddok was nowhere to be found. But I'm telling you people, don't count that man dead."

Partlow listened with interest, but did not show it. So, the thought, the man I want to kill is missing. He must be laid up somewhere wounded. Partlow determined that he was not leaving until he killed Haddok or knew that he was dead. He also knew that if they were searching the country, it was important for him to stay off the land as much as possible. He paid up and left. When he got back to camp, he gave himself ten days. Then he would get back to the business of killing Haddok.

**H**addok didn't mount up until he was on top of the hill behind the ranch. The ranch hands had told him that most of the notched shoe tracks were in the west. He would begin his search in that direction.

As the sun came up, Reed was about a mile from the ranch, nestled down in some rocks on an outcropping shaded by cedars. His field of view was good. It would be nearly impossible for anybody to see him unless he moved enough to draw their attention. Reed studied the land below and marked in his mind the avenues a person would take if they wanted to stay out of sight.

There were two groups of trees and low brush that ran west to east with enough cover to conceal a careful rider. And there were numerous draws and low areas that ran back toward the mountains to the south. A man could possibly work his way through them and get to a place where he could keep an eye on the ranch. There were also two ravines that stood out as deep depressions and Reed could see the tops of trees and brush that grew down in them and reckoned them to run about thirty feet deep. He thought that this area would be the kind of approach he would use if he was the killer. There were a few open places along the bottom of both that Reed mentally noted and planned to glass frequently during the day.

From first light until late in the day he scanned the country side, but there was no sign of anyone. This job was going to take a lot of patience. The only movement Reed spotted all day were deer, a coyote, and birds. He was being real careful. This man is good, he thought. He's been on my ranch for weeks and nobody has seen him. That thought caused a chill to run down Reed's spine and he hunkered even further down in the rocks.

Reed was using his eyeglass well back in the shadows to keep light from reflecting off it. The day was almost gone and he had nothing to show for it. That is, until something caught his eye in the bottom of one of the ravines. There were a couple of open places that he had kept a close watch on and had glassed this one a moment earlier.

Reed almost passed over it. It was close to sundown and he knew it was a time the killer would be moving if he was using one of these routes.

Something was different down there from the last time he had looked. There was a line on the ground that hadn't been there before. The earth had been disturbed enough that light was reflecting a slight color change in the soil. A rider had crossed that clearing while Reed's eyes were elsewhere. He swore to himself and focused on some bushes. Then got lucky. A horse had just flicked its tail as if shooing a fly. Then there was something else in the bushes. A brief puff of smoke. Then another. This feller was smoking a cigarette.

Then the smoke stopped. Reed scanned the ravine ahead of the man but could find no other place where he could see the bottom. It was getting dark.

Reed then leaned back against a rock and made himself a detailed map in his mind how he would get down to that ravine. If this was the killer, and he could think of no other explanation, then he had only been looking for one day and hit pay dirt. Reed's plan was to wait a while and then go down and have a look. He had to be sure.

In a couple of hours, Haddok slowly led his horse toward the ravine. It felt good to walk. He was still not at full strength from the wound. Stopping often to listen and catch his breath, it took about a half hour before he was close to the ravine and the spot where he had spotted the man.

Reed tied his horse and walked slowly to the edge of the deep cut in the earth. The sides were steep from years of runoff and erosion. He eased up and down the banks until he found himself in thick brush. Reed tried to be quiet, but he knew he was making too much noise.

Making his way east, he came to the opening in the ravine. He had to be careful. He slowly breathed in the night air but smelled no wood smoke. In the moonlight Reed could make out some low clumps of grass growing on the ravine floor. He pulled off his boots and proceeded in sock feet, stepping from one clump of grass to another until he got to where he thought the tracks should be. Bending over, balancing on a clump of grass, Reed struck a match. Looking closely, he saw what he had hoped for—one of the shoes was notched on the back right edge. Reed blew out the match, let it cool, and stuck it in his pocket. He then backtracked to his boots, stopping to comb each clump of grass with his fingers so the grass would stand up straight.

Climbing out of the ravine, Reed took his horse and headed back up to the high ground where he would dry camp for the night.

Reed Haddok had to do some thinking.

Haddok slept for a couple of hours and then woke up to listen to the night sounds and make sure his horse was calm. He had the best nose of the two of them. The big black was quietly cropping some grass and seemed relaxed. Reed quietly rolled out and took a few steps so he could look out over the sprawling terrain.

There was a half moon and no clouds. Reed breathed in the crisp mountain air and looked below, scanning the dark tree-covered slopes and mountains, looking for any sign of a campfire. Nothing. It stood to reason the killer was camped close by. Reed then returned to his bed roll and covered up for the next round of sleep. He was feeling stronger each day, but the healing wound in his side still left him weaker than he wanted to be. Sleep was important.

Reed was up at day break and had his glass up scanning the approaches to the ranch. Back and forth across the area produced no sign of movement. Reed was almost certain the killer was already at his post.

Reed's plan was to sit tight until late afternoon and then move down to take up a position in the ravine he had spotted the man using yesterday. This man was more than likely using different routes but, Reed thought, if I am lucky, maybe he will come back down that same ravine tonight.

The sun was halfway down when Reed headed to a point about a quarter of a mile from where he had seen the man yesterday. He quietly moved down into the trees and brush and quickly located a faint trail. The scrub trees and brush were thick with dead brush and limbs laced into the green growth as a result of some flash flood in the past. These ravines could be mighty dangerous to a man caught in water rolling from a rain miles away.

Reed settled down in a patch of brush where he had scraped the ground free of anything that would make a racket. All he had to do now was wait and see if he was lucky again.

It began to get dark and the wind was completely still. That would help. Reed hoped the killer's horse would not smell him. Suddenly there was the sound of a hoof striking some small stone. Haddok came to his knees, rifle ready. He strained to see into the darkness and sensed movement out in front. Then there was the sound of a horse in the sandy bottom and the faintest silhouette of the horse and rider appeared. The horse stopped. Reed thought, has he seen me or has his horse warned him? Reed then heard a slight rustling sound and in an instant a match flared as it was raised to light a cigarette. In that brief glow Reed got a good look at the face of the man who was trying to kill him.

I could kill this man right here, Haddok thought. He wanted to do just that. However, it was not in him to shoot from ambush, even though the man Reed was watching would not have thought twice about it if the tables were turned.

The cigarette glowed in the dark and Reed could smell the burning tobacco. In less than a minute, the killer dropped the cigarette and moved his horse forward. Reed listened carefully and realized he was not heading on up the draw. He was going up the opposite side. A few seconds later and he was gone. Haddok would have to wait until daylight to trail him. Quietly he returned to camp and rolled up for the night.

The next morning Reed was back and carefully tracked the horse up out of the ravine and through a stand of trees split by a small stream of water. It measured about fifteen feet wide and no more than a foot deep.

106

The horse tracks led into the stream and there were numerous tracks along the bank leading in and out of the water.

Haddok waded into the water, being careful to leave no tracks. The stream bed was solid rock and the water was clear. He quietly moved along in the water for about an hour when he decided he had better turn back. Reed didn't want to be seen until he was ready.

He had been backtracking downstream for about ten minutes when he saw it. The trail was back against the grain of the stream and wouldn't be seen by anyone going upstream. The thing that caught Reed's eye was the scarred moss on the rocks behind the bushes that flanked the stream. This trail would have gone unnoticed by anyone less experienced in tracking.

Reed then left the water about ten feet upstream from the trail and followed it from the side, careful to leave no sign of his own. It led up a hollow with steep sides that held a small trickle of water one could easily step across. Back up the hollow a few hundred feet Reed found the camp. There was a shelter and two fire pits, one holding the smoldering remains of last night's fire. The second was stacked and laid in. It was ready for a match.

Reed thought, this feller is a man who really thinks things out. He rides in here at night and doesn't have to fumble around in the dark. Reed thought about the camp for a minute or so and then chuckled to himself. The thought that had run through his mind had painted a picture that he would have enjoyed watching. If I was back in Texas, Reed thought, I would go up on one of the bluffs and catch me a rattler. I'd cut his rattles off, tie him to these fire logs with some piggin string, and wait for this dude to squat down to light his fire. Just the thought of hearing him cry out in the dark almost brought an audible laugh from Reed's throat. But he was not in Texas and he hadn't seen a rattler in a long while.

It wasn't in Reed to just shoot the man and he didn't think he was in no shape for a fight. Getting a fix on the sun, he figured he had about five hours to get back to camp, get his horse, and ride back here so he could meet this man face to face. He was ready for that.

Back at camp, Reed saddled his horse, rolled up his gear, and headed for the killer's camp. He then left his horse tucked into a patch of trees well enough away so the killer's horse would not wind him.

Meanwhile, a plan had taken shape in Haddok's mind and he was satisfied with it. A lingering thought he could not pin down finally materialized in his mind.

Reed quickly made his way up behind the killer's camp. He had about an hour before dark and needed to make good use of it. He began to circle the camp out about thirty paces from the shelter and had not gone far on the high side when he spotted a boot print on the ground. Turning up hill, he walked in that direction about fifty paces. Reed saw what he was looking for.

The sack was hanging from a limb about head high and it was partially concealed by brush. Reed pulled his knife and cut the rope. Inside the sack was a pair of trousers, a shirt, a few cans of beans, some matches sealed in a bottle, and two bags of tobacco.

Reed had grinned when he found the sack because the thought kept running through his mind that this man was too careful not to have a stash somewhere in the case of an emergency. He shouldered the sack and headed for a place near the stream that led to the camp and hid it where he could pick it up later.

It was getting on to dark as Reed settled into a spot behind the shelter and set in to wait. About thirty minutes later he heard the first sound.

The shadow of the horse and rider moved like a ghost through the camp. Reed heard the rider swing down, unsaddle his horse, and drop the saddle just outside the shelter. He then led the horse out to a rope stretched between two trees where he tied him and Reed caught a glimpse of him as he headed down toward the stream.

Reed's hair was standing on edge. This man is a skilled killer and here I am setting smack in the middle of his lair, he thought.

Without a sound, the man suddenly reappeared as if out of nowhere. Reed swallowed quietly and watched as he moved over to the fire pit.

He leaned over the wood and struck a match, lit the kindlin and flames flared up. He then rolled a cigarette and lit it, breathing the smoke in and blowing it into the smoke already rising from the fire. A few moments later he picked up a pot and went to fetch some water. He returned and took what Reed figured was a hand full of coffee from a sack, tossed it into the pot, and set it close to the fire. He then shed his coat and sat down to roll another cigarette. Reed could make out his rifle, a long barreled one, lying across his saddle.

Haddok let him finish rolling his smoke and light it. The sound of the hammer on his rifle as it clicked into the cocked position sounded like a stick of dynamite going off. The killer was startled and jumped a mite before he got control.

"If you as much as think about going for that rifle, or moving your hands for that matter, you are one dead man," Reed said. He offered no movement at all. "What's your name?"

The killer had never been in this spot in all of his days. "The name's Reubin Partlow," he muttered in a shaky voice.

"Well, Mr. Partlow, you've got yourself in a mighty big spot of trouble. My name is Haddok."

"Haddok? The name don't mean nothing to me."

"Then why have you been laying up on my place for nearly three months? I'm afraid you signed on for a job that was a little too big for you."

Reed slowly came into the open. What he saw almost made him feel sorry for the man. He had a haggard look about him and his face was hollow.

"I ought to shoot you and walk away right now. You are the worst of all the sorry and low down men I've ever seen. A man who will lay up and shoot somebody from ambush don't deserve to live. I know it was the money that brought you here. It's not going to be worth it for you."

"What are you going to do?"

"Oh, I'm not going to do anything unless you make me. All you've got to do is move one time without me telling you to and I'll kill you. I really hope I don't have to though. I'm going to give you a chance to live. Now, come out of them clothes."

"You don't expect me to . . ."

The blast of Reed's rifle and the swishing sound of the bullet as it passed close to his right ear got him going. He started pulling his clothes off as quickly as he could.

"Boots, socks, drawers, everything you got on. Get them off and toss them onto the fire."

Partlow looked like he wanted to say something, but he didn't. He just piled his things on the fire and watched vacantly as they blazed up. He stood naked by the fire, his gaunt body a pitiful sight.

"Set down," Reed ordered and walked over to his horse, never taking his eyes off his captive, and saddled up. Reed then took his rifle and looked it over. It was a breech load fifty caliber with roll up sights. The barrel had to be close to forty inches long, heavy and no doubt a deadly long range rifle. He opened the breech and saw that it was loaded before he rummaged through the saddle bags and found about fifty rounds of ammunition, some jerked beef, and tobacco. Reed closed the bags and walked over to the shelter, returning with a blanket and ground cloth which he tossed onto the fire. He then turned to look the man in the face.

"I'm going to give you a chance. It's something you would never have given me."

Partlow looked up, his face a white mask of fear and pleading.

"I would get no satisfaction out of killing you. Just looking at you makes me sick. You could live a thousand years and never be a man. I'm going to leave you here with absolutely nothing but what you came into the world with. I'm going to give you the opportunity to grow up again."

"You can't leave me here like this," he protested.

"It will cause me no pain. You'll have the chance to survive, if you have the guts. That's the chance you have never given to others in your lifetime and I'm sure there are a lot of dead people to prove it."

Reed then took the reins to his horse, thrust his rifle into its scabbard, and started walking.

"Please! Don't leave me like this."

Reed turned around at the outer shadows of the fire. "I'm going to leave your rifle down by the creek with one shell in the chamber. If you are lucky, you may be able to shoot something to eat. If you get out of here, you better stay under cover because I'm telling my men to shoot you on sight."

111

Reed smiled and left, stopping only to retrieve the sack he had stashed before heading for his horse.

Partlow waited until everything was quiet. He then took a stick from the fire and used it for light as he scurried up the hill. The night was getting cold and his body was shaking. He thought, I'll kill him yet. He must have thought I was too dumb to cover all the possibles. His mind was still telling him how smart he was when he reached the tree and the cut rope. His hope died there in the cold night air.

Haddok was about a mile away when he heard the boom of the fifty caliber rifle. He had expected it. I knew there was no man in him, Reed said to himself.

On the way to the ranch, Haddok thought back over the past few months. His life had been in constant danger for too long. He tried to think of when he last felt safe. He wasn't indulging  self pity, simply confronting the fatigue that comes from constantly living on the edge.

Reubin Partlow had been a challenge to his very being. There was a part of him that had wanted to hang Partlow from a tree or skin him alive. But if Reed had given in to that feeling, then he would have been no better than Partlow. Instead, he had chosen to ride away and give the man an opportunity to live. It's one thing to calculate, hide, and shoot a man in the back. It's another to have the courage to live when all odds are against you. Haddok's whole life had been based on surviving with what you've got.

Reed's thoughts went to Loyd Beecham and the pain he had brought into his life. He then let his horse set its own direction, fighting fatigue and the urge to sleep. A weakness began to creep over his body from all his thinking. He pulled up, took his canteen, and splashed water on his face. Then he moved on.

It was after midnight when he rode in. Some of the men were on watch and they came out to meet him.

"How's it going, boss? You find the shooter?" one asked.

"I found him all right. Come on. I'll tell you where you can find him."

They left the horses at the barn and walked to the house. Haddok lit a lamp, went over to a desk, and got a pen and piece of paper. He sketched them a map.

"You'll find him right along here, I expect." Haddok pointed to a spot. "Take a couple of men and go up there tomorrow morning and bury him. I want his rifle. Bring it back."

"We'll head out early. Are you all right?"

"I just need some sleep real bad."

After the cowhands left, Haddok walked into his room, slipped off his boots, unbuckled his pistol, and fell across the bed. As he drifted off to sleep, he saw the smiling face of Loyd Beecham float across his consciousness.

He never knew when Samantha came in and covered him with a blanket, stretching out beside him.

Haddok rode into Prescott about daybreak. Three days had passed since Partlow's death. Two days ago he had ridden home with Samantha to ask for her hand in marriage. He was now on his way to thank Bob Bussler and Sheriff Burgess for their part in helping him stay alive. He headed straight for the livery, deep in thought about the events of the last month or so.

His immediate future included two jobs that had to be done. Both would require time. The first thing he was going to do was find the Indian who had saved his life. Sam had understood his need to do this and to do it alone.

The second was find Loyd Beecham. If he could go back to the day he ran Beecham off the ranch and do it all over again, he probably would do the same thing. He didn't want to ever get to the place where killing came too easy. But Beecham had now left him no choice. Reed was determined he would not live the rest of his life looking over his shoulder. He had a name and a place to start on. After he had found his friend, he would go after his enemy.

Just about then Haddok reached the livery. "Let's go find the sheriff and get us some breakfast," he said to Bob as he dismounted.

It was after dark when Haddok finally rode in at the Rocking H. He unsaddled his horse, rubbed him down, and gave him a bait of grain. He then made his way to the house. Josh and Raven were waiting on the porch when he walked up.

"Well, did Mr. Forbes say you could marry his daughter or did he run you off?" Josh asked with a chuckle.

"He said the only trouble he had with me was the kind of people I hang out with. I guess he meant you," Reed threw back at him, as he pulled up a chair. They talked for about an hour and finally Reed said, "I'm going to go in and rustle me up a bite of food and then I'm gonna turn in. It's been a long day."

"Before you go," Josh said. "I've got something to ask you."

"Go ahead."

"Well, Raven here ain't got no folks. I've just about convinced her to marry me. Seeing as how what I do involves you and what you do involves me, I figured I might make this proper and ask you if I can have her hand in marriage?"

Raven smiled, lowering her eyes. Reed laughed. "Sure you can. I'd be proud to have you for a son."

Reed was up early and after breakfast he headed to the corral and caught up his horse. He had just thrown his saddle blanket across the horse's back and was reaching for his saddle when his hand froze in mid-air. Hanging on his saddle horn was his grandpaw's knife.

He quickly turned and looked around. The barn was quiet and still. There were no footprints on the ground but his own. Reed then hurried to the back of the barn and scanned the flat that ran back to the trees. Nothing! He was just turning to go back when his eyes hit on the damp ground by the water trough. There in the mud was one moccasin clad footprint.

He smiled and walked back to his saddle where he took the knife out of its leather scabbard, turning it gently. It felt good in his hands.

116

News traveled slow in the west. One rider would tell another and one traveler would pass it from town to town. It was told at campfires, church yards, saloons and boardwalks. It was where and how people learned what was going on.

Few stories captured the attention of the people throughout the land like the story of the Texas boy with a price on his head. Haddok was a name everyone knew. People were pulling for him and betting on him all across the west. No conversation lasted long without mentioning the boy from Texas. The portrait of how he had captured the heart of a land could best be described by the unknown rider who rode into a small town along the New Mexico border with Texas, The rider tied his horse at the rail outside the saloon, walked through the swinging doors slapping dust from his clothes and declaring with a loud voice, "Well, he ain't dead yet."